THE VOYAGE OF THE KAZU MARU

A NOVEL BY
LINDA QUIRING

CCB Publishing
British Columbia, Canada

The Voyage of the Kazu Maru

Library and Archives Canada Cataloguing in Publication
Quiring, Linda, 1944-, author
The voyage of the kazu maru / by Linda Quiring. -- First edition.
Issued in print and electronic formats.
ISBN 978-1-77143-564-2 (softcover).--ISBN 978-1-77143-565-9 (pdf)
Additional cataloguing data available from Library and Archives Canada

Front cover artwork: Totem poles in the British Columbia island of Haida Gwaii.
Haida poles, some of which are 300+ years old.
Picture © Kimberly Nesbitt | iStockPhoto.com

Publisher: CCB Publishing
              British Columbia, Canada
              www.ccbpublishing.com

DEDICATION

To Bill, patiently standing by to help, and Paul, a great publisher!

Also, family and friends who encouraged me and especially, Michael Igo, for his input!

Prologue

Henri Picard, known as the foremost scholar in France on Asian and Buddhist history, opened the ancient manuscript before him cautiously; its pages brown and withered with age. Curious at first, he became more excited as the document revealed its secrets to him. Found recently at the venerable Asian Studies museum in Arles which was being reorganized and rebuilt, it seemed no one in recent memory knew how or when the script had arrived there, but it was believed to be several hundred years of age.

As Henri sat in Paris where the scroll had been sent, he spent hours reading in growing disbelief and amazement at what he had discovered. Finally, hunger drove him to leave the pages made from traditional Japanese washi and return home for the evening. That night, unable to comprehend the import of the tale which revealed itself, he had wondered if it was the manuscript of a book some erudite scholar had written after a trip to the Far East. Or was it indeed written by someone from the Orient in an attempt to provoke and mystify his audience.

Finally, Picard called in colleagues from his years at the Sorbonne, to help verify the contents of the ancient pages but mostly to share with them his excitement at finding news that would surely reverberate around the globe: A voyage to the coast of North America and back by a monk in a small fishing boat hundreds of years previous to all known voyages across the vast Pacific Ocean.

Part One

THE MOUNTAIN

Chapter One

"Too many!" screeched the old lady, her voice harsh in the morning light.

"Too many!" She meant boys.

Small boys were everywhere, shouting and pulling at each other's pigtails. Some were kicking an old block of wood around the courtyard, over ground smoothed by centuries of straw sandals shuffling in and out of the monastery.

Half hidden in an isolated grove, the dark brown wooden buildings were scattered with needles from the strong and silent trees surrounding them. The ancient pines and cedars standing on the mountainside were already old when the first thirteen-year-old initiate, his pate fresh and shining, had received his monk's robe and bowl.

Once solitary in its mountain home, the wooden temple with its high arching shingle roofs now sat at the very edge of a small settlement which had grown through the centuries to surround the monastery. Behind the old village, small gardens rose in terraces to the very edge of the forest.

Rarely in contact with the outside world, the venerable temple hovered in a remote valley deep in the forested hills of a vast range of mountains. In spring the rush of water could be heard from streams and creeks that flowed down the mountainside, and ancient pathways led the monks and villagers off into the forest to lakes and meadows hidden in the mountain fastness.

Tradition taught these same monks that eventually the

mountain paths led down, ever down until they reached the sea. The concept of open ocean was just that however, as not one of them had ever made the journey. It was only in stories overheard from travellers and passed down through the ages that such a thing even existed.

Mist and fog rolled in occasionally, and often vicious winds they all knew came from that same sea, for the scent of salt and sea was carried amidst the clouds and rain, although the sea was hidden from view of the village by the surrounding hills.

The old lady gestured to the tallest of the boys, perhaps twelve years old. As he neared she handed him a basket of green vegetables and daikon that she carried over her arm, and then walked resolutely towards the entrance court.

"Ichiro," she said, and pointed at the brass bell that hung to one side of the intricately carved wooden doors.

Although small and frail, bent with age, Kiku stood with dignity before the door and motioned the boy to strike the bell and summon the shika or guest master. The boy Ichiro hung his head, then reluctantly walked to the doorway, grasped the gong and set the bell pealing.

The door opened presently and an aged monk smiled at the old lady, bowed and touched her shoulder gently.

"Arigatou gozamasu," he said, thanking her for the offering, then glanced at the boy.

Tall and thin, the old monk was stooped with age, his face a map of weathered skin deeply penetrated with lines and wrinkles. Yet behind the almost paper-like aged visage lie two bright eyes, almost startling in their clarity and intensity. He smiled at the boy.

Old Chogun, the guest master, recognized the boy from his strolls through the village and even knew him by name.

"Ichiro." He nodded towards the boy.

"Come," he said, then gestured and welcomed the two into the zendo. The monk of course recognized the lady; one of the local householders who supported the monks with donations of rice, vegetables and herbs grown and gathered in the nearby forest and hills.

Kiku had been born to the peasant class and spent her early years on a nearby farm. At a young age she had begun service as a domestic in the home of a prosperous merchant in the village and here she had spent her adult life. When both the merchant and later his wife passed away, Kiku had fallen on hard times.

She now lived in a small dwelling that had been part of the merchant's estate and close to the nearby temple. Thus, Kiku lived and worked on her small patch of vegetables surrounded by the comings and goings of the entire village and zendo, including the ragged patch of boys who ran back and forth on their way to school and played noisily in the lanes and courtyard.

Among the boys was young Ichiro whose father had left for the wars and never returned. His mother Tsuya had died suddenly of the fever and since then, Ichiro had been left to forage for food and care among women of the village but in these times of dearth and want, he often went hungry.

Thin for his age, his arms and slim legs lost in dirty rags which hung loosely from his body, with thick dusty hair and now a frightened look in his eyes, Ichiro bowed his head.

Ichiro was rootless, living now at one home, then another as circumstances changed; a new child in the family might mean no bed for Ichiro and again he would be homeless until taken in by someone else. Quiet Kiku however, always seemed to have a mat on the floor available for Ichiro and would feed him as he came by, even when he lived elsewhere.

Perhaps it was that she had never married or had children of her own that she had become so attached to Ichiro but now, as he grew taller and out of his boyhood, she knew he must have a future and this she could not provide.

Old Chogun, who would stroll to the village market to purchase food and other supplies which were not donated by families living close by, had begun to notice the boy more often. One day, he saw the youngster had become thinner and more ragged, and asked the boy what he had eaten that morning. Ichiro just shrugged.

"Nani mo Mai," whispered the boy, afraid that he had done something wrong.

Now, Kiku quietly but firmly requested that she speak to the Roshi! Duties were rotated monthly among the dozen or so monks still living there and so the one who responded to the bell changed often. Removed in every way from the venerable order of monks to which they had once belonged, the twelve who now dwelt in Shirakawa lived in accordance with traditions which had shifted over millennia.

Old Chogun had been one of the first young village boys to become a monk those many years ago and was now a venerable old master himself. His father was Samurai and had perished in the battles that once terrorized the native peoples as bands of marauding brigands sought out even the small, faraway outposts of Japanese civilization lost in these distant hills.

Chogun knew even before Kiku could voice her strange request to the Roshi why she had come. The boy would soon grow into manhood and she could no longer feed or clothe him. Also, he had reached the age when young boys might be taken into the monastery to begin their rigorous training as a Zen Buddhist monk.

"Come," said the old monk, then kindly and gently took the

boy's hand and led him slowly back to the low buildings in the clearing.

"No! No!" shouted more than one of Chogun's fellow monks as they walked through the old, dank halls amid more shouts that protested the breaking of traditions laid down centuries before and rules that should not be broken. The old monk just shook his head and led the boy to a small bench near the kitchen. Chogun knew the temple and its order of mendicants could not continue to exist without patrons to provide food, clothing and shelter and that a healthy connection with those villagers must be maintained.

Chogun glared silently at those who continued to grumble, then turned to the kitchen where food was being prepared for the imminent noonday meal.

"Here!" He handed the boy a bowl of rice which he ladled out of an earthenware pot and pointed to the rest of the meal.

"Go!" he continued, and the boy looked hesitatingly at the others. Some were leaving in protest. Some just shrugged, knowing the will of Chogun was immutable. The boy began to eat, refilling his bowl often as his benefactor looked on in approval.

Chapter Two

Once inside the zendo Ichiro looked about, fascinated by what he was seeing. Access here was limited and almost no one from the village had ever seen the living and working quarters of the monks, only the temples where villagers joined in prayers and meditation. Everywhere, it seemed, was the aromatic smell of incense.

A loud gong suddenly reverberated throughout the zendo by a monk wielding a heavy mallet and Ichiro, startled, looked towards Chogun for assurance.

"Time to eat!" Chogun smiled. Ichiro would soon become used to the sound of bells and gongs, for all happenings in the zendo seemed to be announced this way. Five times a day the bell pealed; for wake up, to eat, later dinner, meditations. Soon these sounds became just a routine part of life, like walking or breathing.

It was now mid-morning and time for the main meal of the day, and Ichiro was led to a low bench with a tatami mat before it and an empty bowl sitting on the bench. Chogun motioned the boy to sit cross-legged on the mat just as others in the room were sitting. Soon this mat, six feet long and half as wide, would become Ichiro's home as he slept, ate and meditated upon it.

The others in the room looked quietly at the boy; some with mild curiosity, others wearing frowns at the audacity of old Chogun in breaking with tradition. Usually young men were apprenticed by their families after many consultations between parents, the monks, and finally, the young man himself to make sure he did indeed have a vocation and was not just in need of food or a home.

Lunch was a delight for the hungry lad! To him it was a strange combination of sweet potato, boiled chestnuts and his favourite, mushrooms from the forest!

Startled, Ichiro noticed a familiar face across from him. Dashiro had been a year or two older than he but unlike Ichiro had grown up in a large family. The two boys had played together years before, Kamari usually, in front of the temple gates which had the smoothest ground.

One day, Dashiro had just disappeared and soon the other boys heard that as he had been so bright, performed so well in his studies and had such a fervent wish to join the monks in the zendo, his parents had taken him there to live.

As one or more monks could be seen daily walking the village streets, they were a familiar sight to the boys, with their deep and large bamboo hats, their straw sandals and cotton leggings.

Once a month or so, a group of two or three monks would walk through the village on their begging rounds, although in truth these occasions had nothing to do with begging. It was a practice that would help the monks develop the attitude of humility they must cultivate.

The monks would visit homes and businesses and would chant sutras in exchange for food and money. This was not begging, as in this ritual, there was no giver and no receiver so no thanks were given. On occasion, they would visit the nearby fields for donations of wheat, pumpkin, turnips or other vegetables.

Yet the boys knew these quiet men were somehow different; that they must be awarded a high degree of respect by all. Each child knew from a young age that they must be quieter when in their presence, that they must make way for the monks in the streets and nod to them if eye contact was made.

"Sit down," said his father Hiragana the day after Dashiro turned thirteen years. He looked stern and for a moment Dashiro was afraid he had been too loud and boisterous at his birthday meal.

"You are a man now," Hiragana continued, "and so now you must think of work! You are grown and must help the family."

Dashiro breathed a sigh of relief; he was not in trouble, but... Help the family??? Work???

"You must find work. We cannot feed you any longer. You must go to the fields."

"No...?" Dashiro hesitated. A life in the fields was never a vision in the future he had planned. In fact, he had never thought of his future, just assuming his life as it now existed would go on indefinitely.

"There is another way," said Hiragana.

"You could go to the temple!"

Dashiro's uncle had joined the zendo at a young age and thus a precedent existed in the family. When the zendo was offered as an alternative, Dashiro had a sudden vision of himself, just like his uncle Hirosada, walking through the village in a manner different from others and set apart.

Dashiro quickly agreed that a life of asceticism was his wish, although at thirteen he did not fully grasp the importance of the step he was taking. Now, he is a humble apprentice, but has come to love life in the zendo.

Ichiro is suddenly comforted by the presence of Dashiro and after the meal is finished, smiles and walks towards his old friend.

"Greetings," he says.

Dashiro smiles, but does not speak and turns to follow the line of monks who now leave the room and return to their practice. Ichiro will soon learn there is no talking at mealtimes.

"Come," said Chogun with a smile, and leads Ichiro into what will be his sleeping quarters for this next chapter of his young life.

"Do not worry," said the old monk when they are out of earshot of the others.

"You will have much time later to meet with your friend."

Next day, falling in line for the mid-day meal, Ichiro finds Dashiro close behind him.

"Fun!" said Dashiro in a loud whisper.

"We will have fun!"

"Just do not make noise in front of Roshi! Or a big stick will come!"

Dashiro laughs, although Ichiro is still too intimidated by the monks to respond due to the formality and discipline of the zendo.

The next few days and weeks are a fascinating time for Ichiro. At times he is angered by the lack of freedom which he has lost. A sunny afternoon makes him want to join in the faraway shouting he hears occasionally from the village as the boys shout and yell at their games. He has grown up too fast.

Other times, Ichiro feels for the first time since early childhood, the comfort of his own bed every night; the knowledge that each meal will be there on time to assuage his ravenous young appetite. There is great kindness from most of the other monks; older by far, who realize what the youth is going through, having all experienced the insecurity of being drawn from their homes to live in the zendo and attend the temple.

Ichiro is surprised to find that he misses old Kiku and for the first time realizes she had kindly replaced the mother he could now hardly remember. Scenes of his early childhood race back into his mind on these first cold, lonely nights spent on his mat amongst older men he had not known.

"Douzo," she said quietly. It is his mother Tsuya, offering a four or five-year-old Ichiro a handful of cherries picked in early summer. It was a beautiful sunny morning and Ichiro and his mother walked to the market. His heart was filled with warmth, then sadness and longing as Ichiro realized this is just a dream, a memory, and that his mother has been gone these many years.

Away from the noisy life of the streets, Ichiro finds more of his lonely childhood returning to conscious thought: the sadness and loneliness he experienced when his mother died from the fever.

"Komodo wa doko!" Where is she? He cries when he realizes his mother is gone and will not be back. The two younger children are scattered between relatives, friends and neighbours as is the custom in these days, but not until kindly Kiku takes him in does Ichiro have anything like a home or family.

Now, it seems perhaps he has finally found one. As Chogun predicted, more and more often it seemed he and Dashiro would be working together; peeling vegetables in the kitchen under the direction of Masato the cook, washing robes in buckets of hot water or other simple tasks that needed doing.

One day, walking from the zendo after sitting, Ichiro saw the cook waving him over towards the kitchen. His spirits soared as he knew Masato usually had small chores for him to do; tasks which were enjoyable and easy, unlike the onerous tasks that might be given to him by others.

Once in the kitchen, Masato pointed to the far corner under

the large wooden table where Ichiro had now sat countless hours, peeling vegetables or cleaning rice. Beneath the table sat huge baskets of rice and barley that were served daily, and Masato pointed to several baskets that were only half full or less.

"Here," he said. "Take this!"

He turned to a nearby shelf and picked up an object that jolted Ichiro into the past with an almost physical reaction. Ichiro recognized the abacus Masato held as identical to one his father had handed him often as a small boy of perhaps three or four.

Ichiro knew it was not merely to play with. He had seen his father time and again sit quietly with the abacus; the wood faded from decades of handling. Katsumasa had shown him how to move the beads back and forth, but had not been there as Ichiro grew to help him learn the intricacies of the abacus, as common as the broom in every home.

Masato pointed at the baskets, handed Ichiro a cup and asked that he count them; that the grains were running low and Masato needed to know how many servings remained. Perhaps it was time to walk through the village and receive offerings from the householders to replenish the supply.

Ichiro shrugged his shoulders and shook his head. The old cook gazed at him with eyebrows raised, the question unspoken.

"No," said Ichiro, looking down at his feet, feeling ashamed.

"I do not know it."

This was unusual for someone his age, just another thing he had missed growing up a waif, except for old Kiku who either did not use the abacus or just had not taught Ichiro how to use it.

"Hmmmmm," murmured Masato, now smiling kindly at the boy.

"Something for a rainy day!"

He gestured to Ichiro to just measure out the grains with the cup. Time flew happily by with these simple chores and endeared the old cook to the nervous boy, almost like the father he had lost so long ago.

Today, it was Ichiro's day for cleaning rice. Sitting on a small wooden stool, idly looking out at a tiny bird attacking a dry plum hanging from a branch nearby, Ichiro suddenly heard loud cracks and bangs, voices shouting.

He looked quickly to Masato for assurance; that all was well, that no trouble was afoot in the usually peaceful surroundings of the monastery. Masato caught the quick worried glance and instantly smiled at the boy.

"Kenjutsu," he said with a grin.

"Just kenjutsu!"

Ichiro knew the name for the ferocious martial arts he had seen practiced in the village and now recalled the time all the boys gathered noisily in the courtyard had heard a sudden cacophony coming from behind the temple gates. Sticks; crashing, clanking. Shouts of victory. Wails of frustration. Yes, the monks had been practicing their kenjutsu also, as younger men in the village often did.

Masato grinned and said, "You can learn."

He moved so suddenly to the door that Ichiro was momentarily afraid, of what, he knew not. But the old monk just grabbed a broom that leaned against the wall and began to wave it before Ichiro, yelling the calls of victory as he spun and circled a silent boy in pretence of a fast and furious bout of kenjutsu.

As Ichiro grasped what was happening, he laughed and laughed, then nodded as he understood Masato's offer to teach him the skillful art of defending oneself, of scattering one's enemies. Then, they were both laughing as Masato handed

Ichiro the broom, nodding to him to come at the skilled old cook.

Soon, they would be spending an hour each day or so in the courtyard, thrusting and banging with the sticks fashioned from bamboo as Ichiro learned the intricacies of this ancient martial art. From old Chogun he learned in their far off youth, both he and Masato had been adept in the practice; that indeed Masato had been well-known in all the land as a venerable master.

Another shift in Ichiro's days and life as he left behind more of his boyhood and moved towards being a worldly young man. And, he loved the practice! Ichiro could feel his confidence rising, along with swelling muscles, a stronger gait, the steadier balance in this new and more powerful body. Someday, Masato assured him, it could save his life!

Gathering mushrooms soon became Ichiro's favourite chore out of many. The freedom of running through the open woodlands nearby and even occasionally the dark forest looking for a sudden flash of white, or the more subtle brown of a different mushroom became an exciting quest. But mostly it was just the feeling of freedom, away from the overly strict discipline of the zendo; harsh for such young boys.

More and more often now it seemed he and Dashiro would be sent to work as a team on some project; hauling wooden buckets of water to various spots in the temple or wiping and polishing the ancient wooden floors of the great temple to a soft, brilliant shine.

Ichiro knew that somehow Chogun had something to do with this and felt a happy smile whenever he encountered the old monk. With others around, Chogun could be very formal and strict. The first time this happened, Ichiro felt he had lost a friend and ally.

"Not today!" Chogun laughed when Ichiro grabbed a broom as he appeared, smiled and took the broom from Ichiro's hand

and placed it against the wall.

"Today we go to market!" His voice carried a depth of humour and laughter that warmed the heart of the young boy.

"You can carry the basket!"

Weeks and months went by in this fashion and his old life began to recede further in his mind as the life of a Zen Buddhist monk became the new reality.

Chapter Three

For a young boy, the change in his daily life was so overwhelming, Ichiro hardly had time to ponder what was happening. Each day began early with a bell calling the monks to wake up. Ichiro now spent most of his waking hours it seemed, practicing Zazen in the small woodland Soto, or on occasion in the vast meditation hall which many years before had held a hundred monks.

The days passed and he fell into the rhythm of the zendo; the times of prayer, meal times and the time for chores. At first, sitting on his mat for long periods frightened Ichiro. Each sitting lasted for two hours, much of it stationed on his heels and during the chanting, Ichiro was racked with alternating bouts of boredom, pain and sleepiness.

Sometimes, the stick would fall heavily on his shoulder as he actually fell asleep and slid soundlessly to his mat.

Sitting still, doing nothing, not allowed to even yawn or move to adjust his position, his mind would be drawn back again and again to his childhood when forgotten incidents of his earlier life would be recalled.

"Bad boy!" His father's voice was loud and harsh when he found Ichiro playing with Makaze, his sharp sword and trying to pull it from its sheath. The memory still froze him with terror and now on the mat tears came to his eyes and Ichiro felt the sharp gaze of Katsumasa upon him.

Or those fleeting memories of his mother would return without warning; the warmth of her arms when returning home after a trip to the market. A broad smile spread across his face as he sat, daydreaming when he should have been diligently practicing the mindfulness that he must cultivate to become like the monks who surrounded him.

"Here, try this!" She had reached in her market basket and pulled out a strange-looking item that turned out to be the sweetest thing Ichiro had ever tasted.

Often, he fondly recalled old Kiku tending to his needs, although he could not recall how this came to be. As he grew older, some days she would send him to the rudimentary village school but mostly, she would teach him herself; reading, hand-lettering the characters one must learn in order to write.

Walking in the village one day with Masato, baskets slung over their shoulders, Ichiro saw old Kiku coming towards him with a sweet smile on her face. She bowed towards Masato, and then took Ichiro's hand.

"Here," she whispered.

"This is meant for you." Kiku handed Ichiro a bundle of cloth; old worn silks, scarce in these times. Ichiro felt in it something hard and long. Unwrapping the folds, what he saw took his breath away. It was his father Katsumasa's Samurai knife. The sword Katsumasa had carried off to war but this smaller knife or tanto had remained behind.

The tanto had been kept in a place of honour and Ichiro remembered once taking it down and handling it, only to hear his mother's voice telling him sternly to put it back upon the shelf. He realized now that when his mother died, old Kiku must have rescued the tanto and kept it until Ichiro was grown.

Ichiro looked to Masato, who only nodded, letting the boy know that it was permissible to accept the family heirloom and the young lad placed it carefully in his basket. Somehow, he felt this was a very important moment; something linking him to his family and his forefathers. Ichiro then realized he had not one single treasure from his previous life. He thanked Kiku again and again, then smiled and waved as Masato took his arm to lead him on.

"How do you do it?" asked Ichiro. It was the first time the boys had been alone; sent by the cook to wash vegetables in the courtyard.

"Do what?" laughed Dashiro. He knew Ichiro would be as nervous and strained as he was upon arrival at the zendo.

"Like it here!" replied Ichiro, the look on his face both puzzled and annoyed.

"Don't worry," Dashiro laughed softly, looking around him to make sure no one was watching them chatter.

"You'll get used to it."

"They try to be harsh at first," he continued, "to let you know they are the boss."

Only Masato seemed to know how to amuse the boys with his funny stories about daily occurrences in the kitchen, like the day a huge raven swooped down and flew away with a roasted fish that was cooling on a tray. The boys drifted more and more to the kitchen whenever they were not called by the bell to sit or do other chores in the temple.

Ichiro soon learned another rule of life in the zendo: No work? No food! Soon he was out in the woods with Dashiro and one or another of the monks; chopping wood for the fires, then carrying it back to the kitchen slung on two bamboo poles.

With the cook's help, he was learning to plant herbs and vegetables in the small garden which they tended behind the kitchen, cleaning mushrooms gleaned in the forest after a rain and setting them out to dry in the heat of the afternoon.

But mostly, his time was spent sweeping; inside, outside, with the wide straw brooms. Strangely, Ichiro began to enjoy his chores, especially the sweeping where he could spend an hour or two alone, in quiet contemplation of his new life. Then, monks passing would just nod, with no order to do this or that; to be anywhere or do anything else at all.

"Not now!" Matsumoto screamed at Ichiro, who had approached him to say that his mat had become drenched after a sudden rain where it had been hanging outside to air. Matsumoto was one of the monks who felt the taking in of young homeless boys who had not been called, made the zendo into a kind of orphanage and he and old Chogun had had words about this more than once.

Yet other monks seemed to sense how frightened the boy was and to make small gestures to make him feel safe and at home. Perhaps they recalled themselves at thirteen, lonely and insecure in the vast empty halls after life in a small, crowded home filled with parents, siblings, friends and neighbours.

Meals were a welcome respite from the rigorous training in the temple, with quiet whispers and sometimes even soft laughter from the others.

But foremost, he must practice now in stilling his thoughts. Once, a startled wakefulness as the calm watching of his thoughts and stilling the mind actually brought him to a new dimension of the depths inherent in his own being; that there was more to him than his thoughts. A new life began of asceticism; of constant practice and discipline.

"I spoke with Roshi." Chogun's voice was unusually quiet.

"He says you are much too young for initiation and it will be several more years until you are grown. You must think like a man to also make this important decision. So, work in the kitchen will keep you busy for now."

Dashiro had explained some of the workings of the zendo and so Ichiro knew Dashiro was being prepared to have his initiation at some point.

Ichiro nodded and said, "Yes," but felt just a bit jealous that his older friend would now have a much more important role in the zendo than his own place in the kitchen. Yet, as time passed Ichiro would begin to think the mundane chores of the kitchen were preferable to the rigors of the zendo.

"Come with me," Chogun said and motioned as he appeared near Ichiro's mat one morning.

Ichiro knew that Dashiro went each day into the zendo to practice zazen. Ichiro did not really understand why the monks did this or what they were doing, although he had had glances inside as he carried water or performed his now routine chores.

On the walk towards the meditation hall, Chogun explained that although Ichiro was too young for formal training or initiation, Roshi thought the practice would help Ichiro 'grow up' as Chogun explained.

Ichiro had seen the very old Roshi several times and once in passing had overcome his fear and looked Roshi in the eye. Apparently this was not a good practice, as thirteen-year-old Ichiro would soon learn. Roshi's stern glance taught the boy to look humbly down at his feet in passing and then to stand silently by.

In the coming days, Ichiro was sent time and again to the zendo by Chogun or old Masato who would delegate chores to Ichiro. Somehow, Ichiro instinctively grasped that the chores were a kind of test and that if he performed well, a reward would come.

Now, more and more often the cook would send Ichiro to the zendo when the floors were scrubbed clean, the daikon peeled and washed, the wooden bowls wiped clean. This began to happen at least once each day or two and soon Ichiro was learning how to quietly sit for hours cross-legged on his mat.

Taught how to breathe just so, Ichiro would practice again lying on his mat in the long dark nights, knowing that performing well in the zendo was rewarded with kindly nods by the other monks, while nodding off as he occasionally did, was greeted with dark looks and scowls.

Ichiro learned that as Roshi had decided he was too young for initiation, Ichiro was not given his koan to study but that at some time, if he persevered in his practice this might happen. Occasionally, Roshi would give a formal talk but again Ichiro would have no understanding of the esoteric teachings that came forth.

"Humility!"

Ichiro's desire to please was mostly to avoid the dark looks, the hostile mutterings from those monks who still resented Chogun's challenge of the rules by harbouring Ichiro in the monastery. So Ichiro one day had asked old Chogun what he was to learn by sitting.

"A life of service!" continued the old monk, pleased that Ichiro was actually interested in why the monastery would exist at all and the reason for practice.

"Work!"

"Labour!" Chogun barked another day when the cook complained that Ichiro had been a bit lazy that morning. In fact, his time in the kitchen had been arranged by the two old monks who just enjoyed each other's company and had decided kitchen work would not only keep Ichiro out of trouble but placate those who still had animosity towards the whole arrangement.

"Prayer, gratitude," came another day after a question by Ichiro after a walk in the village where a householder had filled their basket with a huge handful of fresh ginger.

But again and again, Chogun's message was that a life in the zendo was a life of meditation and slowly this foreign concept became more and more clear to the boy.

One day, walking to the village with Chogun, as happened more and more these times, with Ichiro carrying home a basket or two of vegetables or rice, a strange moment of calm and thoughtfulness occurred.

Ichiro perceived that it was not just a strong arm that Chogun wished from him, but that it was another form of teaching, as they usually talked as they went along. Today's calm chatting by Chogun gave Ichiro a sudden perception or understanding that he had become a student of the old guest master.

"Tell me, why are you here?" The question had come to Ichiro unbidden and quietly slipped from his lips.

"Here?" questioned the old monk. "Here?"

"In this village? At the zendo? Here on this earth? I do not understand?"

Here? Here? What DID he mean? Ichiro thought deeply about what he wanted to understand… no, it was not… why do we live in this particular village.

"Here," he repeated. He thought again about how to ask exactly the question he wished to understand.

"My father," he continued.

"He was a soldier; he went to war to defend us from the marauders coming through the forest. He never returned." Ichiro breathed a sigh of remorse.

"My uncle," Ichiro continued, "he was a farmer. He grew rice and barley. His farm was behind the village."

"There!" Ichiro pointed upwards and over to the fields.

"Uncle too left for war and never returned!"

"I see," said Chogun quietly.

"And you are wondering, the men of the village all work, they all have a family to feed, they spend their days at hard labour while we in the zendo are just sitting on a cushion? Daydreaming?"

His voice became a bit harsh, thought Ichiro.

"No, No!"

"I do not ask that," said Ichiro.

"But, but, what...?"

"What are we doing?" Chogun stopped walking now and looked directly at Ichiro. His voice was soft.

"We are doing the most important work of all!" He smiled faintly.

"We have given up a home, a wife, a family. The games, the gathering with friends, the drinking of ales? Why? Why?"

"Man needs to know who he is. Not the man of earth, but the inner man, whom no one ever sees. Most men do not know this inner man. Your father Katsumasa, a great Samurai knew who he was; the inner man."

Chogun looked away towards the hills, a faraway look in his eyes.

"It sent him off to war," he continued. "To give up his family to defend not only our village, but our way of life from the brigands."

"We sit in the zendo, quiet, alone with ourselves, our souls, to divine who we are. Why do we live? We commune with the inner man who tells us how to live! To bring the wisdom of the great deities to life in our humble selves."

"We do this, not for ourselves," Chogun went on, "perhaps we are a heavy man who eats too much, or one who is too lazy to work, but for all, for us all who need to know the value of a life; who we are, why we are here; to do the will of the higher power we meet within."

Ichiro breathed in suddenly; a deep gasp of air as he realized during this talk he had been holding his breath. Chogun looked at Ichiro in a strange way, not happy, not serious, not angry, but with a strange gleam in his eye. Suddenly, he smiled at Ichiro, turned and walked on.

Ichiro would never forget this day.

As he sat now on his cushion, a new world surrounded him; one full of the deity he might find within, if only he was quiet enough; if only he could conquer the constant thoughts that twirled and whirled around in his head. The thoughts of his sad life, of being an orphan, alone. No home. No mother.

It seemed a large hand now grabbed him, squeezed him tightly and held him there for a long moment. And he saw his sadness, his whole being self-absorbed in pity. And now for all time, each of these thoughts which passed before him, he would conquer.

Sitting in the interminable silence one morning; cold in the early morning air, just as he felt himself sliding into sleep, a vision appeared in his memory.

A moment from his childhood: Ichiro may have been three or four.

"Katsumasa!"

It was his mother calling his father's name. A stranger had appeared and Ichiro's mother had walked into the room where his father was sitting in silence. Ichiro suddenly remembered following his mother and seeing his father sit; immobile and distant, as though he were somewhere else, although his eyes were clear and sharp.

With a start, Ichiro knew his father too had sat, and after this experience, he went to the mat with an attitude that was different. Strangely, he now felt that sense of gratitude Chogun had spoken of and felt fortunate that he was allowed in the zendo with the authentic monks when he was just the washing boy.

Slowly, though, Ichiro noticed his relationship with Dashiro was changing. At first, Dashiro had treated him as a younger brother, showing him things, teaching him about life in the zendo to keep Ichiro out of trouble.

"You stupid!"

The first time Dashiro yelled at Ichiro he was taken aback, his feelings hurt. They had been ordered to carry mats and cushions from the dojo outside for airing. As the younger boy struggled with his load, some items had fallen on the dusty ground, incurring the wrath of Dashiro.

Ichiro had felt for days that their easygoing relationship had somehow changed and indeed, it had. Dashiro had begun to envy what he felt was a special relationship evolving between old Chogun, Masato the cook, and Ichiro; that they were treating him in a special way.

At the same time, as Dashiro was deemed more grown-up and mature, he was given more responsibility for Ichiro. He was now told to take the younger boy with him on errands to the village; to show him how to take care of his meager belongings, his mat and bowl.

Ichiro could sense the resentment and tried different ways to appease Dashiro but somehow a shift had occurred between them which would now always be there in the background of each encounter.

Chapter Four

"Too busy."

The cook shrugged his reply when Dashiro inquired one warm spring day if they might go fishing. The other monks always gave a cheer when warm fried fish appeared at the midday meal.

Dashiro had often gone with Masato to a small stream that ran down the mountainside and through the woods from a distant lake high in the hills. With great patience, a degree of skill and fresh worms dug in Masato's small garden plot, fish could actually be caught in an eddy that pooled amongst some huge rocks and boulders.

"Too busy," repeated Masato.

"Take Ichiro with you!"

Dashiro grinned from ear-to-ear at the idea of this new freedom. Collecting the lines and nets used to catch the fish, he dashed into the courtyard where he had last seen Ichiro raking fallen leaves beneath the soft shifting light of the cherry blossoms.

"Fishing!" Dashiro yelled. "You can come fishing!" Once again the two were just friends, all jealousies and resentments forgotten at this rare privilege; a chance to just be boys away from the stern discipline of their daily lives.

"Come," chattered Dashiro excitedly! "I will show you!"

Grinning with pleasure at this unexpected day of freedom, the boys ran happily through the woods. Everything here was foreign to Ichiro; the ever-narrowing, steep path between the towering majestic pines, the song of a strange bird.

A sea wind thrashed the tops of great cedars and occasionally, a strange shape or sound emerged from the woods. Some of these Ichiro recognized: a silent deer browsing on native bamboo in a small clearing, several feral rabbits and once a raccoon familiar from their raids in the village gardens.

"Boo!" Ichiro jumped! Dashiro had suddenly shouted in his ear.

"Bear!" He laughed. Both had been warned as children about huge bears which roamed the forest, but now ever more rare.

Two years had passed since Ichiro had joined life in the zendo and he had just turned fourteen years old. Dashiro was sixteen however, and had recently had his initiation. Curious, as Ichiro expected one day to do the same, he wanted to know all about it as they trudged along beneath the spring blossoms, ever more slowly as the path grew steeper.

Dashiro would meet personally with Roshi, he revealed, and this always threw him into a state of nervous energy. He had been given his koan by Roshi but also had been yelled at and once slapped by him when he had been lazy in his sitting.

This day in the forest somehow made Dashiro yearn once more for the freedom of village life and he suddenly wondered: how he had come to be a monk?

As they walked along they saw even in April, vestiges of snow in deep, dark places. Occasionally, there were bursts of spring colour in the dark paths of the forest from the lavender blooms of the woodland azaleas. Often they walked under the fresh young green of wild cherry leaves after the fall of the pink and white blossoms and once a small valley of Japanese maple, the light-filled red and bronze leaves fluttering in the breeze.

Turning a bend, Dashiro suddenly yelled!

"Matsutake!"

Ichiro too, recognized the patch of five or six huge mushrooms that lie in their path. He remembered the enticing smell of the sizzling fungi being cooked over the fire after his mother had been at market. Less often, she would just come home from somewhere with a clump of the delicious morsels in her basket.

These big mushrooms sometimes appeared at the table when monks walking in the forest or foraging in the fields in late spring or after fall rains stumbled upon them. They were considered a delicacy, sliced and fried or occasionally stuffed with rice or vegetables if the cook was so inclined.

"Ha!" They both laughed as they picked the largest and stuffed them into their packs as an extra bonus to perhaps serve with the fish they would catch.

Then, a sudden view of sharp peaks amid a formidable ravine which the path luckily skirted at a dizzying height. They had been walking for hours. Once, they stopped for a quick dip in a small mineral pool swirling amidst the streambed where small silver fish could be seen ascending the stream.

Here in their homeland, earthquakes, some mild, some causing horrendous damage were familiar to the boys; first a distant rumble, then the ground shaking beneath their feet. Centuries of quick shocks to the earth had left small mineral springs scattered throughout the mountain ranges. Here and there, they encountered a small shrine placed between towering majestic pines and once, beneath a hoary old cedar larger than Ichiro had ever seen. Sometimes, just a stone specially placed upon another. They did not stop to venerate each shrine, as they knew they should.

Then finally their destination unfolded before them! A great waterfall came tumbling down out of a hidden ravine into a small pool which swirled slowly before leaping several hundred feet down. After a particularly difficult climb, they were over a rise and there in front of them, a cool, clear mountain lake; more water than Ichiro could ever have imagined.

Out came nets and lines and the two boys stood amidst an amazing viewscape of mountain peaks and calm water with sunlight gleaming on its placid surface. Their hearts were full.

"Yattaaaaaa!" shouted Dashiro as the first silver fish came flashing to the surface.

"Here," he had shown Ichiro just how to set a line, then how to handle the net when a fish caught hard. The first time this happened, Ichiro was so excited he felt he could not breathe!

The day's fishing had been exuberant fun and they had just been two boys laughing and flinging their nets, their lines, with shouts of excitement and joy when a small fish was caught. Hours later, tired but happy, the boys walked through the silent forest each with a string of fish over his shoulder.

"How many?" Ichiro asked again, knowing they had twelve fish with them but wanting to hear the number again and again. Dashiro just laughed. As they entered the hall near the kitchen though, they heard old Chogun's voice; most animated for him.

"Come! Come!" He gestured and there in front of the boys were three men, the first they had ever seen not from their own small village. Each was wearing a long outer robe, with a small bag draped over their left shoulder and the usual higasa or woven hat. Ichiro could see a pair of spare sandals draped over the shoulder of one of them. Chogun was welcoming them like old friends and tea had been set out.

"Kakudo." Chogun pointed to the oldest monk. The boys instinctively bowed towards him.

"Utsumi." The second monk smiled more benevolently.

"Kanjun." Chogun introduced the third, then all sat for tea.

Dashiro and Ichiro both knew from stories and old tales that strange monks would suddenly appear in the village from time to time; part of a band of marathon monks known as gyoja, who had once frequented the village on their runs through the forest.

Later, fairly quiet from their exhausting day of adventure, the boys were working in the kitchen scaling and cleaning fish under the eye of Masato when Chogun appeared and graciously thanked the boys for their hard work and diligence to bring the fine dinner home for all to enjoy.

Especially, he thanked them on behalf of the running monks who, it appeared, had not had such a meal in weeks. Chogun took some time as they worked to explain their presence to the boys.

Known as running monks, they had descended from powerful lords. Once, huge temples and monasteries had covered the mountainside, of which some had been burned by warrior monks in olden times. Temples might include lay monks, workers and warrior monks in those far off times and often, there were wars between different factions and temples might be burned or destroyed.

Old Chogun went on to explain that mountain pilgrimages on sacred peaks were the best of practices, with organized pilgrimages of 100 days, some of 700 days, and the ultimate of 1000 days of constant running. A marathon monk is one who has completed five 100-day runs. They are then given a white belt to wear and thereafter may use a staff to help them negotiate their way through the mountains.

Chogun became more excited as he spoke and the boys knew they had been in the company of a different kind of monk. As they listened, they both gained an immense amount of respect for the three whom they had just met.

Chogun continued, "They run and live under the pines and on top of cliffs. They wear the pure white outfit of the Gyoja, and carry a small bag which holds their handbook; this contains the knowledge and wisdom they seek."

"It is all very formal," he continued. "They chant continuously!"

"The bag you see on their right shoulder contains their handbook, candles and matches. On the left shoulder, the bag carries their food. And you will see, over their shoulders as they run are more straw sandals, as the ones they now wear will fall apart over their long journey."

"On this journey, they will face storms and heavy rains in the wet season, their sandals will disintegrate in the mud. Their robes will never dry out!"

"They are on a search for enlightenment! They will stop at sacred peaks, hills, stones. They will run through forests and stop to chant in bamboo groves, when among cedar and pine trees; at ponds, streams and waterfalls. After the run, they will be fasting for nine days; no food, no water, no sleep. They usually live in caves and grass huts."

"However," Chogun explained, "Kakudo, Utsumi and Kanjun do not practice formal running. Rather," he continued, "they believe in study and practice, and not so formal running."

"Wild monks sleep on a mat. On this mountain they once lived in caves and huts. They ate herbs and mushrooms from the forest; nuts and wild vegetables, occasionally fish."

The two boys were fascinated. Stories had never been told to them of life outside their small isolated settlement, apparently once a bustling centre of religious life.

"They commune with the sun." Chogun paused and a

faraway look came into his eyes.

"With the sky."

"With the earth and spring water." His faraway look told the boys that he too, perhaps might have wished this life. Chogun left then and the boys were now silent, contemplating the strange life of these mysterious running monks.

The three running monks spent several days at the monastery, taking part in sitting at the zendo, eating meals with them. To Dashiro and Ichiro, it seemed a subtle change had come over the temple. There was more talk, more laughter; a less formal atmosphere, which suited the two youths.

Then one morning, Dashiro heard Kakudo speaking with Roshi.

"No, no!" he insisted.

"We must go now!"

"Please," Roshi insisted.

"Very well," responded Kakudo.

"One more day!"

When Dashiro reported this conversation to Ichiro, both sat for a time in silence. Both thought of the fun and excitement the running monks had brought to their highly disciplined lives; the stories, the laughter, the tales of previous runs.

"I want to go!"

Dashiro spoke suddenly, his voice filled with enthusiasm.

"I am going!" He spoke with conviction.

Ichiro stared at him in silence. Dumbstruck, not even able to imagine such a thing ever occurring. His eyes widened.

"Then I am coming, too!"

The two boys sat in stunned silence, not sure of this new reality. Could this really happen? Could they really leave? Run down forbidden trails? Leave their old lives behind?

"We will need to make plans," said Dashiro, immediately taking charge. He then told Ichiro what to do, which clothing to take and what food to grab. A plan was made. They would leave with the running monks in the morning.

Chapter Five

Dawn broke over the distant hills, the sun pale and weak under a thick blanket of mist. Two exhausted but excited youths sprung from their mats, having hardly slept.

"Shhhhh…" Dashiro held a finger to his lips. All must be done with the utmost silence. According to their plan each left at a different time, staggered so as to not arouse suspicion among the others that anything was amiss: that nothing out of the ordinary was happening. Separately they slowly made their way to a small gate that separated old Masato's garden from the temple.

Behind the tall cedar fence, they retrieved the belongings they had hidden in darkness the previous night. Dashiro had been adamant that they take only what was necessary; just the bare essentials to preserve life. Gathering his meagre food stores, Ichiro hesitated when he saw Kasumasa's tanto, then thrust it quickly into his bag.

As arranged, they met further down the path in an area close enough to still be familiar. Ichiro arrived last, as planned.

"Dashiro?" His voice was a whisper.

"Yes!" came the soft reply. "I am here!"

They waited, chewing on pieces of cooked fish leftover from their catch. Suddenly, they heard voices, then footsteps.

The running monks were not running but walking at a leisurely pace, each with his belongings strung over his back in their cotton bags. They too were eating, having left the zendo before the morning meal. Talking as they walked along, unaware when two young shadows blended into the dim woods behind them, not close enough to see or hear them.

An hour or two passed.

"Look," pointed Ichiro.

Footsteps, traces of marks left by straw sandals were scarcely visible on the dirt pathway. In some places, sword ferns and mosses covered the trail so rarely used and no trace was visible, yet the boys knew from the monks' tales, there was only one way down through the trees.

The journey was said to take three days of constant running at a set pace.

Then, the sun broke through to reveal a magnificent peak covered with towering forests, steep ravines and thundering waterfalls off in the distant east. This whole landscape was cut off from the world by heavy mists in summer and deep snow in winter. Bamboo groves came into view, amid the forest of ancient cedar and pine.

Later came the sudden sound of rushing water, then a roar as a narrow stream of water fell hundreds of feet down as they, too, descended the mountain.

Once, beneath the oldest cedar either had ever seen, the roots came to an abrupt stop just a foot from the pathway and at its base, on a plinth made of rock sat a stone Buddha with traces of ash still left from where the running monks must have burned incense.

"Shhhhh!" Dashiro's whisper came just as Ichiro began to speak of something in the forest.

"Shhhhh!" he repeated, putting his finger to his lips. And Ichiro could hear it! A soft, melodious humming coming from deep in the woods before them. The three monks were chanting,

chanting as they ran along and again and again the boys would recognize this faint sound. It served as a warning that they were perhaps getting too close to the running monks and might be discovered.

All day they ran. Young, strong, and healthy, they moved easily through the woods, careful to not make noise; to move silently. Always, they were aware of the possibility of running into those three before them.

"Wait! Wait!" shouted Ichiro the first time his friend jumped up and quickly disappeared down the path leaving Ichiro to stumble clumsily to his feet to try and catch up.

They ate as they ran along; rice balls wrapped in small cotton squares and precious chunks of leftover dried fish gave them energy to run for more hours. Water was found everywhere along the path in streams, even as trickles of spring water running down the mountain alongside them.

Thankfully, it began to grow dark; early now in spring. The boys were tired, exhausted even, and wondered how old Utsumi could outpace them.

"Stop!" whispered Dashiro, who always ran in front.

A small, sharp point of light flashed through the trees in front of them. Dashiro again held his finger to his lips and motioned Ichiro to crouch down in the grasses alongside the pathway as he was doing.

"Yes!" whispered Ichiro. They could now hear a short laugh, a cough from time to time; voices coming through the dark night.

The boys slept fitfully, afraid they might be found by the others or that they might make a noise and their hiding place be discovered. They found that upon awakening, the fresh mountain air would certainly clear the head.

Morning came with a soft light among the trees and the boys woke to heavy fog blanketing the mountainside. Listening, they heard no sound and slowly began to make their way downward, slowly at first lest the monks hear them. Soon, they found remains of a small fire with coals still warm from the night before; the source of the light they had seen.

"Eat!" Dashiro whispered and they soon realized their stores would not last them for two more days.

They ran.

All day, they ran.

"Aaaiiiee!" cried Ichiro. The sharp edges of rocks and points of roots on the trail were beginning to cut his tender feet to the quick. They stopped often to grab handfuls of dry grasses left from the autumn winds and stuff them into their straw sandals.

Down, ever down. They could not have imagined that they had spent their lives at such great altitude. On and on they ran. Ichiro's legs and tendons began to throb. As the day wore on, he felt a strange warmth creep into his bones, beginning at his feet. This, perhaps, a slight fever from the punctures in his feet which may have become infected.

Yet, once or twice Ichiro felt himself one with the mountain, flying along the path on their swift downhill journey.

By late afternoon both Dashiro and Ichiro were becoming dehydrated and streams and ponds became less common. Ichiro's saliva began to dry up and soon he could taste blood in his mouth, but on he ran until they found a quiet trickle in a stream bed where he could rinse his mouth with cool water.

"Gone," said Dashiro, his voice without emotion.

"All gone."

They had come to the end of their meager food supply and

from now on it would be wild vegetables, early spring berries, even pine needles and if lucky, some young bamboo shoots and dandelion greens.

Thankful now for the approaching dusk, they slowed down as there was no way to know whether the three elders running before them had stopped for the night. A clearing in a small grove beckoned and they stopped to rest. No longer did they fear losing sight of the others, for they found the path leading down and down, with no byways to lead them astray.

Instantly, they both fell into a deep sleep.

"Aaaaiiieee!"

Startled, Ichiro awoke to a loud scream from Dashiro, who was standing, arms flailing, with Kakudo holding him upright.

"Go back!" Utsumi's voice was adamant.

"Go back!" he repeated.

"Do not follow us!"

Kakudo let go of Dashiro, who struggled to regain his balance, then replied, "We are not following you, but going down the mountain!" He sounded afraid.

"Where then are you going?" Utsumi was not impressed with this answer.

Dashiro did not hesitate, although his answer was an absolute falsehood.

"Ichiro's father disappeared to the wars, down to your village, and never returned."

Ichiro could not believe the outright lie and how quickly Dashiro had manufactured it. He could see Utsumi hesitate. He turned to Ichiro.

"What was his name?" he demanded.

"Katsumasa," replied Ichiro. "Tanaka," he continued.

He revealed his mother Tsuya once telling him his warrior father had set off for the wars and never returned, which made him a hero within the small village.

At this, Utsumi was satisfied.

"We cannot feed you," he said, looking at the boys sternly.

"You cannot come to the monastery," he continued.

Both boys quietly nodded as the running monks turned and walked away down the path.

This day of running was like none other. There was now no fear of being detected; no reason to hurry or hesitate. As the day wore on they sensed a newfound freedom; for the first time in their young lives completely on their own, to do as they may.

"Look! Look!" shouted Dashiro, still in front, although sometimes this day, they ran down the path together as it widened out.

The path had led them to the remains of an old temple; dilapidated wooden buildings with roofs caved in, some piles of wood which were partly burned, remnants of what must have once been a great hall.

During their visit to the zendo days earlier, the running monks had spoken about deserted temples in the forest; great monasteries burned in the wars where different religious factions attempted to vanquish one another.

Once, Ichiro felt himself gasp: in came a sharp breath, and then slowly out as shock at the sight before him turned to amazement, then wonder. Another Buddha, this one large, sat on a granite rock, smooth and flat. Just as he approached this inspiring sight in the midst of a dense, isolated forest, a deer had slowly stepped into sight from behind the statue.

It stopped; seemed to sense that something was there and slowly moved its head towards Ichiro. Two large brown eyes looked at him, seemingly with full knowledge that he was a young human who would not harm him, then turned and slowly made its way across the path and quickly disappeared into the forest.

Ichiro felt his breath slowly and calmly; in and out, in and out. Somehow the two, deer and boy, had touched each other in the soul, spoke to each other. This life was beginning to move into another phase, where Ichiro was becoming one with all around him; the friends, the monks, the birds and wildlife, the great forest itself.

"Rain is coming," Ichiro predicted.

As the day wore on, the boys became more and more familiar with the forest around them and the sky ahead. It seemed they could now predict the weather from the shape of the clouds, and from the direction of the wind and the smell of the air.

Their country, always wet with rains, became a lush green world in spring. Down, down they ran. Then finally, dusk penetrated the forest. They had not passed the others, but could not help but admire the three elderly monks who had bested them in the marathon journey down the mountain.

They also felt very proud, as Kanjun, who had told the zendo monks that the journey took them three days, had also said that ordinary people took five or six days to cover the same distance.

Night fell and once again they rested in a small depression by the path's edge, close by another worn stone Buddha nestled in the hollow roots of an old cedar. Darkness closed in upon them.

Chapter Six

Dawn came. A fresh breeze moved the highest branches of the cedars above them, yet down below the path was still. Gathering their lightened bags over their shoulders, the boys began the day.

Down, down, and the pathway began to change and became much less steep. As the morning wore on the vegetation also began to change; more wildflowers, the cherry trees here had already shed their blossoms and had leafed out into pale green. The cedars were less frequent and younger and the pines had disappeared with fir and hemlock taking their place in this wooded universe.

Ahead of them, traces of the three monks were still evident; a clump of straw which had escaped a sandal, the faint scent of smoke from the previous night's fire. Soon a new and strange sound began to pulse in their ears. Slowly at first, then with increasing volume, a dull thunder could be heard in the far distance.

They slowed down the frantic pace they had kept up for days, sometimes to the point of exhaustion. The dull noise grew unabated, nearer and nearer they seemed to approach this strange new phenomenon.

"Ocean," pronounced Dashiro. Amongst the stories told from millennia in their isolated village was that of a great body of water which lie at the foot of their mountain range that issued a constant booming sound; that this sound could prevent one from even sleeping.

Suddenly, in front of them stood the three monks; standing

still before a statue sitting on a huge rock. From marks across the base the boys could recognize it had been smoothed and flattened with stone tools.

"Ohayo!" greeted Utsumi. "How are you?"

Smiling ferociously at having vanquished the mountain and seeing the wide grin of the old monk, the boys shouted with happiness.

"We are fine!" shouted Dashiro and watched as the monks turned down a narrow side path which wound around the side of the enormous Buddha and then continued into the woods.

"Our temple!" Utsumi pointed to that narrow path. "You cannot come!" he continued.

He then directed them to continue down the path they were on. Utsumi assured the boys they would meet again at the small village which they would soon discover lie just ahead.

Again, the two sped up their pace, fascinated that they alone would actually get to witness such a mysterious force of nature the booming sounds predicted. The sound became ever louder and more rhythmic; it pulsed in a constant tide of louder and softer tones.

Then, around a bend in the widening pathway, a sight which stunned them; left them standing together in stilled silence at the scene which lie before them. There in front of their eyes lie the largest body of water either of them could have ever imagined. Like the hidden lake on the mountain where they had been fishing; was it just days ago? Another lifetime!

Yet this body of water was without end, stretching into the farthest distance. On the right lie a thrust of land, curving around and outward, then nothing. Only the water which now lie in front of them and seemed to flow inward and outward before them: the origin of the booming sound, but now a roar.

"Yattaaaaaa!" They both shrilled at once, waving arms and running, rushing towards the tide, slowly rolling in and out before them. They stood transfixed for long minutes taking in the unimaginable scene before them.

They stood at the head of a large bay. To the right lie the long curve of land they had seen, with a strange wooden pathway built out over the water. They had never seen a pier before. To the left another curve of land, encircling a vast distance where the waves slid into infinity.

They sat for an hour or more.

"Look!" one would point. A great strange seabird soared overhead.

"Look!" the other would shout as a fish jumped nearby and always, the great thrum of the surf in front of them. After a time, they noticed the waves receding into the distance. Puzzled, they thought perhaps this strange vision would disappear into the far horizon.

Then, a small object appeared in the distance and moved closer even as it bounced up and down upon the waves. They watched, transfixed as it moved nearer and nearer. It seemed a large flag waved from a tall post.

"Boat!" Dashiro shouted. "A boat!"

He had heard about such wooden craft that men could build and that would magically float on water. As it neared, the boys could see a diminutive figure moving about, carrying something from here to there. Eventually, the boat approached the end of the wooden platform.

They ran over the sands to the wooden pier and down along it. It seemed to sway and rock with each large wave, yet their excitement at this new adventure overcame their fear at running over the waves pounding the boards and posts beneath them.

When the boat had reached the end of the platform, they were there and watched as a man in a blue tunic and broad hat took ropes and attempted to tie them to a post. The boards swayed with each passing wave and he was not successful and so gestured to the boys.

"Help me," he called and held out his rope; looked at the end and gestured to a nearby post. Ichiro reached out first and soon the small craft was tethered to the wooden railings which ran down the pier. The man climbed out and thanked Ichiro. Then, he gestured for him to follow as he jumped back down into what seemed a vast mound of netting.

Never had these country boys seen so many fish. And huge they were, some of them, compared to the shiny silver fish they caught. All three, they dragged and dragged and soon filled three large baskets the fisherman had handed them.

"Where are you from?" he inquired, smiling and friendly with gratitude.

"Up the mountain," pointed Dashiro and the man nodded.

"Akihito," he pointed to himself.

"Dashiro," he said, and pointed at his chest. Then at his friend.

"Ichiro!"

Akihito then picked up a bundle from under the board seat which lie across the back of the boat. As he opened the bundle, the boys saw a veritable feast of rice balls, dried fish and pickled daikon. They looked on hungrily as he began to eat. He looked up, hesitated and thrust out the bundle.

"Eat!" They did not have to be asked again and gratefully swallowed the tasty morsels all the while mumbling their gratitude.

"Do you have food?" asked the fisherman.

"No." They both shook heads in unison. Akihito hesitated. Then shook his head.

"No food," he repeated quietly.

"Where do you stay?" he inquired.

The two looked at each other, then at Akihito.

"Come," he said, getting to his feet.

"Come," he repeated.

"You can help." He picked up one huge basket of fish and motioned the boys to do likewise, then gestured them to follow. The three walked slowly up the old wooden pier, across the cool sand to the land and down the shore where small buildings began to come into view; the first of many.

At one he stopped, opened a gate and entered a small courtyard leading to a door. Inside, a diminutive woman stood gleaning barley over a wooden table. Surprised at these new visitors, she immediately made a small bow as Akihito introduced them to his wife, Katsumi.

"Myumi!" he shouted and a door behind the table opened slowly.

"Myumi!" Akihito pointed at the boys in turn. Dashiro, always first, as he was taller and obviously the elder of the two. Then Ichiro.

Ichiro felt his face must be burning. He had never encountered such a beautiful vision in his entire life or even dreamed a girl could be so beautiful. In the zendo, he had soon learned that one did not stare at females they encountered in the village or even glance their way.

That his quickened breathing betrayed these rules only proceeded to heighten his excitement. Her skin looked like satin;

as though if one touched it, it should feel like the finest silk.

"Hello," he nodded awkwardly and bowed his head.

Myumi's hair was brilliant and black; shiny as a new coin, her lips full and soft with a gentle pouting expression. She too bowed, a slight nod and Ichiro perceived a quick change or did he imagine it? A quiver of a different smile, a quick flirtatious look. But mostly, it was her eyes. Never had Ichiro seen anyone's eyes so large, bright and piercing; as though they looked right through into his heart.

This same heart was pounding with excitement and Ichiro felt everyone in the tiny room must surely hear it. He was saved by Akihito's voice.

"Come," he directed and motioned them to follow as he turned and left the house. A few feet behind the modest home sat another, even smaller wooden hut. Akihito opened the door and motioned them inside. The untidy floor was covered with old nets, garden tools, boards, buckets and baskets.

"You may sleep here tonight," he told them and gave simple instructions on how they could fold the nets and store them on some shelving against the back wall. The baskets could be filled with the hand tools and garden implements and the boards piled outside against the back of the hut.

The boys worked feverishly after he had gone; both puzzled at their good fortune in finding a place to sleep and confused about what to do and why. Eventually Akihito returned, nodded in approval at their efforts and motioned them to follow.

Inside the house, dinner had been served on a low table and they sat down cross-legged before it as they had done in the zendo. The meal was simple and humble; fresh fish fried to a golden brown, boiled barley shaped into balls, and steamed vegetables.

"I have no sons to help me," Akihito offered. Both Katsumi and Myumi lowered their heads.

"You can stay here," he continued.

"I am growing older and need help with the nets, the sails."

He nodded towards each of them, both silent and not knowing how, or if, to respond.

"Tomorrow," Akihito went on, "you can help me clean the fish for market. The small and damaged ones, we will dry for winter."

Akihito looked to each of them as if to make sure they were in agreement with his plans for their future. They did not know how to respond and so they did not. With no real plan for their adventure down the mountain, they had never thought about what would happen when they actually reached their destination.

Ichiro would spend the rest of the meal casting sidelong glances at Myumi and trying not to be noticed.

"Katsumi, go and find some mats," directed her husband, "under the old things."

Akihito motioned to some closets and shelves in an adjacent room to the side of the kitchen where they had eaten. Katsumi rose, turned and motioned Myumi to accompany her. After some minutes of sorting and straightening things, they returned to the kitchen with two very old and worn tatami mats and held them out towards the boys.

"Here," said Katsumi and handed one each to Dashiro and Ichiro, both smiling broadly at this wholly unexpected turn of events.

Soon, it was growing dark and after such a full day, the most exciting of their young lives, both boys were ready to sleep almost forever and so they did. Akihito led them out to the hut which would be their home for many, many months. He gave them each a mat and some coverings which he had placed over his arm, foreseeing the cool spring night which would come.

The next day began as so many others would for the youngsters and thus, they began to move into manhood, another past life forgotten.

This village, although small, was unlike Ichiro's home in many ways. Where his village held perhaps a hundred people, this one was certainly at least three times as large. The fields surrounding it grew more and different vegetables and grains; the workers had more and different tools to sow, weed and harvest with.

Up at dawn, the men walked towards the fields carrying their tools, with food and water in bags slung across their strong shoulders. They could be heard laughing and chattering at their work. After a long day, they would meet in groups at the many small tea shops which lined the village lanes and here they would sit for hours until bells or voices called them home to dinner.

There was here, not a small school, but several of them where children from small to almost grown sat in dusty, crowded rooms. Cross-legged on the shiny, worn wooden floors, they held their abacus and slid beads, looked brightly towards those teaching them, listening intently. Ichiro, as he glanced over towards them, often wished that he had had such schooling.

Best of all, which warmed Ichiro's heart, were the village squares where the children laughed and played. Older boys playfully copied the martial arts of their elders, noisily battling with strong sticks they fashioned from nearby branches and trees. Always to the side, small groups of girls played; the little ones scooting small wooden balls across the square. Older ones would glance his way and giggle as he and Dashiro walked by.

Now, each morning when the boys awoke, they would wash in a basin of cold water set on the bench outside their hut.

After a quick meal with Akihito, served by Katsumi, with the elusive Myumi nowhere to be seen, he and the boys would walk with baskets, nets they had repaired, and some bundles of food down to the boat. It would be tied to the dock with other small fishing boats, surrounded by busy chattering fishermen also setting out for the day's catch.

Akihito's small boat was like most others; five or six metres long and what seemed to Ichiro, quite wide at the beam. A small deck ran several feet across the bow, enough room to store tools, nets, and other gear. Midway along ran a bench and another at the stern where the boys could sit and eat, mend nets or chat as they drifted along waiting for a catch.

Two long oars were stashed along one side and a cranky wooden rudder helped guide them out of the bay towards open ocean.

A wooden pole stood sentinel at the very tip of the small craft, with the canvas sail sometimes tied close to it, sometimes unfurled to catch a breeze. Rarely was it fully let out, unless they were racing home to escape a coming storm or high winds.

With Akihito busily moving about the boat, showing them how to maneuver it in different winds and waves, the boys were soon enjoying their new work as sailors and fishermen.

Some days the weather was inclement: the first time Ichiro encountered bucking waves rocking the boat and a horrendous noise as waves crashed against their craft, he looked to Akihito with fear evident on his startled features.

"We go back now," Akihito said, just nodding slightly, but quickly moved to turn the boat around and head for shore.

Chapter Seven

Ichiro's life as a fisherman had begun and he now knew he would never be a monk living in a zendo. As this thought ran through his mind, he suddenly remembered the honour which that life brought to men, and how at one time he could not wait to be fully grown and walk through the village with friends and neighbours bowing his way in deference to his vocation.

For just a brief moment, he became jealous of this imagined future but a pull on the net brought him to the present moment. With a sigh of relief, he knew he preferred the freedom of a fisherman to the harsh discipline of the zendo.

Now his days were filled with sitting on an old wooden bench in the narrow courtyard behind their hut; mending nets in the slow, methodical but perfect way which Akihito had been doing for many, many decades. Dashiro did not want to mend nets, and so, he did not have to.

A particular day might be fishing and the three of them would walk down to the boat, greet the other, by now familiar fishermen and head out for the day's fishing. Another might be spent on Ichiro's least favourite task; cleaning the smaller fish, removing the innards which he would spread on Katsumi's nearby kitchen garden and hanging the cleaned fish to dry on a line strung across the courtyard.

One day as he sat with the fish, the ground began to move and rumble beneath him. Ichiro had often experienced this and didn't think too much of it as earthquakes were part of life on his island of Japan. There was not usually any damage in his village so he had no real fear of the infrequent rumbling and shaking.

A few days later on a festival day, with no working and no fishing, Ichiro and Dashiro walked along the beach throwing branches back into the surf; laughing and tossing handfuls of seaweed at each other. A seemingly extra big tide had thrown upon the beach much more of the usual detritus. Suddenly, their rough play came to an abrupt halt. There in front of them, harnessed and caught in a trap of seaweed, old fish netting and other debris, was the longest fish either of them had ever encountered, on land or at sea.

Ichiro gasped! Was this the elusive sea serpent one heard about in hushed tales, never knowing whether these tales were told to noisy children to scare them or just to quiet them down? As they stared in amazement, too startled to even touch the strange satiny skin of the fish, they spied one of their fellow fishers coming down the beach behind them.

Turning, they were hailed by Takaya, an older fisherman from the village. Takaya was the father of one of the local boys who had become their good friend despite it having been difficult for them to be fully accepted as part of village life.

"Greetings, young fellows!" he called out, then strolled over to see what they were pointing to with such excitement. As a senior fisher, Takaya knew every fish, mollusk and creature in the ocean.

Apparently, it was not their youth and inexperience that made the fish seem so unusual. Takaya, upon drawing near and seeing the fish with its unusual crest and reddish fins and stripes, looked just as startled and shouted "Oarfish!" He leaned over and slid his hand over the smooth skin, for this fish had no scales.

"Bad omen," he said, and looked around towards the village and the hills beyond.

"Bad omen."

Takaya then explained that these strange fish lived at incomprehensible depths. That oarfish were rarely seen and if they were, it meant trouble, sorrow, and perhaps even devastation for the land. Giant oarfish were apparently well known in local folklore; a harbinger of an earthquake. Rumblings which would predict a cataclysmic event would begin days earlier and the fish, whose normal range was thousands of feet down would flee towards the surface. Rarely, they might be caught in a net. More often, they would be found washed ashore, like today.

"Bad omen," Takaya repeated and shook his head slowly at them before making his way further down the beach.

The boys looked at each other, just shrugged and began to laugh. Old myths about the sea, the fishing, and the strange creatures the sea might harbour were part of local lore and not to be taken seriously.

Unlike his younger friend, Dashiro did not like the life of a fisherman and complained in a regular fashion about his chores. Akihito would just smile and ignore him, or frown slightly if the complaints went on too long.

Other days, and these were the best, Ichiro might accompany Myumi to the market, carrying a basket of dried fish which they would sell. Then Myumi would purchase supplies needed for the household and these Ichiro would carry back.

In the mornings, women sat in groups before the small cottages, weaving baskets in many shapes and sizes Ichiro had not seen. In his village there were only two or three shapes in various sizes. The women laughed and chattered, most nodding to the young man as he walked by looking in their direction.

Myumi was quiet and shy at first, and would hardly look at either Ichiro or Dashiro. But as the weeks and months passed, she began to talk with the boys, then, to laugh and smile at their antics and silly jokes. These times made Ichiro's heart sing! He knew that he was in love with the quiet but flirtatious Myumi and would someday marry her. Often he would have dreams about her and wake smiling, knowing he would soon see her lovely face across from him at the table.

A new family unit had now formed in the small home, with Akihito treating the boys like the sons he had never had. At mealtime one day, he told the boys that as he got older, injuries he sustained decades ago were beginning to bother him more and more and indeed, he did always walk with a slight limp.

"You will have the boat," he said, nodding to them each in turn, "and I will not be fishing soon."

Katsumi nodded as if in agreement with this and the boys had noticed more than once that there seemed to be some embarrassment or sadness on her part; that she had not produced sons to help with the fishing.

There were also, at mealtimes and other casual gatherings, subtle hints that brought a twinkle to the boys' eyes and later a giggle, that Myumi would soon be of an age to find a husband. Two years passed in this fashion and now Dashiro was a young man of eighteen with Myumi a year younger and Ichiro a year younger still. The old jealousies which had plagued the boys years before had now unfortunately returned.

It was obvious to everyone that someday, one of the young men and Myumi would become man and wife. But which one? With all the masculine attention from the competing youths, Myumi had become more and more flirtatious as time passed. She would smile at them coquettishly now, and they in turn began to bring little gifts to her; a flower from the courtyard, a brightly coloured feather from an exotic bird which Ichiro had found in the village one day.

As the days went by, Ichiro's heart grew full. There were

many times when he and Myumi would be alone together, usually when the others were away. Katsumi might perhaps go to the market with her basket to purchase vegetables. Akihito would be fishing and Dashiro might be with him, or more and more often, also in the village spending time lounging around the tea house or just the streets with other youths his age.

On these days, as Ichiro sat with his chores; mending nets, preparing the smallest fish for drying or turning over soil in the small kitchen garden, Myumi seemed to appear more and more by his side. At first, he was nervous about being alone in her company, not knowing how to act. Yet over time, Myumi herself set an atmosphere for their time together; laughing and giggling at his adolescent attempts at humour. Over time, Ichiro became more comfortable in her presence and eventually even bold enough to put his arm around the willing Myumi and place a hesitant but soft kiss on her cheek.

Here in his new home, a trip to the village was exciting. Tables set with baskets of fish, daikon, weavings, clay pots, sweet rice cakes and more. Groups of elders in their robes stood in clusters; laughing, chatting, arguing loudly at times. A scene familiar from Ichiro's village, but so much larger, noisier, more vibrant and alive.

Returning from market one lazy afternoon when Ichiro had walked more slowly than ever before so as to prolong his time with the dazzling young woman of his dreams, a thrilling experience lie in wait. It was Myumi herself who beckoned Ichiro to leave the path and walk over to the wall of a boat shed nearby. Here, to Ichiro's delight and coupled with a nervous dread of something strange and new, Myumi paused, then lifted up her long skirt to show her ankle and leg.

She pointed to a small mark or bruise there and began to rub it sensuously. Then glancing slyly at Ichiro, nodded and looked pointedly at the mark. Ichiro, for a moment, did not know how to respond and so just stood there in a rapturous daze. Myumi, looking at him piercingly, then took hold of his hand and guided it to her leg, showing Ichiro just how to caress the mark. Soon, their lips met somehow; Ichiro did not know how this had happened or whether it had been he or Myumi who had taken that first amorous step to romance.

Their lips met again and again and as these were not children but now young adults, Ichiro felt strange and wonderful sensations as their embrace grew more intimate. At each further step, having no experience with love and fondling it was Myumi who led the way, revealing that perhaps she had had previous experience in the art of love.

It was Ichiro himself who finally pulled away, aroused yet confused at being swept away by the current of desire for the first time. Myumi smiled coquettishly at him, picked up her basket and returned to the path, leaving Ichiro with new and blissful feelings for days. Myumi, however, each time he caught her eye, failed to respond in any way but her usual soft smile.

When they returned home after their encounter, Ichiro could feel old Akihito looking at them both with a strange look on his face, both puzzled and perhaps a bit angry. Ichiro felt that each moment, each kiss of their encounter was glowing brightly on his now reddening and guilty face.

Ichiro knew in his heart that they would one day be man and wife. Once or twice, he thought he caught a certain look being exchanged between Myumi and Dashiro, but told himself that Dashiro also yearned after the lovely young woman and to be friendly, she would just exchange a warm glance.

One day, after many weeks of hidden glances, flushed cheeks and soft smiles, Ichiro was once again alone with Myumi on a walk from the village after a gathering in the square. Somehow, they had become separated from Akihito and Katsumi, with

Dashiro nowhere in sight; usual for him as he had many older friends now.

At the first small trail leading into the woods from their pathway home, Ichiro suddenly grabbed Myumi's arm.

"Come," he said softly and led her quickly through the old pines and deeper into the forest. Far enough away from the lanes where they could no longer hear the laughing and chatter, he sat and gently pulled Myumi down beside him.

They lie quietly in the soft green grass, and as Ichiro softly stroked her arm, Myumi leaned against him and began to kiss his neck. Quickly, he pulled her to him and ardently kissed her again and again. Later, Ichiro would wonder that she seemed much more experienced in the ways of love than did he!

This day, there was a fever pitch to their embrace that had not been there before. Long moments passed, their passion growing as their kisses became longer, deeper and suddenly, Ichiro found his hand gliding along Myumi's breast. In a moment, it was though he awoke and was almost frightened by his daring.

Yet, instead of pushing his hand away as Ichiro had expected, Myumi gently touched his hand and slid it beneath the folds of her tunic. His hand grasped her breast closely, firmly, while Myumi felt for his other hand and placed it tightly against her.

Soon, Ichiro was pressing himself closer and closer to Myumi's welcoming body. His breath was becoming faster, faster and deeper when he heard her whisper quietly in his ear.

"Yes!" She breathed. "Yes!"

Now, for the first time, Ichiro felt his manhood arise and strange new sensations roiled his body as his thoughts, mind and feelings gave way to an overwhelming desire to push forward, to consummate this love between he and Myumi, to make it complete. They would be one.

What stopped him, he never knew. But suddenly, strangely, he felt weak... drained from being swept up in the current of desire. Slowly, he let his passion fade and just dreamily stroked Myumi without the passionate fondling and grasping. She merely softened against him and after long moments thus, Ichiro spoke her name quietly.

"Myumi," he whispered. "Myumi."

He began to move, to rustle and to rise to a sitting position and she along with him. Ichiro looked intently at her, inches away, as if to decipher from her large dark eyes what was unsaid by her soft, full lips. But, there was nothing. Just a dazed and sleepy look in her eyes.

Ichiro rose now and took her hand.

"We go," he said softly and led her quietly, silently down the woodland trail towards the village.

In the following days, as Ichiro struggled to absorb that powerful experience; his first fully mature recognition of his nascent manhood, it seemed when with Myumi that possibly nothing at all had happened. She gave no sign, no recognition of their relationship as lovers; no intense looks, no sign. Nothing. Ichiro was puzzled.

The powers of love were new to him. He was unschooled in the annals of love -- a mere lad, ignorant and unskilled. He waited; for what, he did not know. Not for one moment did Ichiro ever doubt the affection he felt was not shared by Myumi, even though he knew Dashiro was becoming more and more jealous of this special relationship.

As time passed, bad feelings began to grow and eventually the two young men could not even work together without harsh words being exchanged. Akihito soon noticed and with his shrewd skills would now delegate them different duties to perform. This, however, would have a dire consequence for young Ichiro.

"You are the best young fisherman!" exclaimed Akihito one morning, when Ichiro pulled in the largest Red Sea Bream that anyone had seen in recent years. They were having a poor catch that cloudy day, with the nets coming up half empty time after time.

"We can go out further," said Akihito.

"Yes!" beamed Ichiro and set sail into the wind. He asked Akihito how far out one could go.

Akihito looked at him strangely.

"Some have gone out so far," he replied, "that they never returned."

Akihito went on, with old tales that had been handed down for generations; that boats were sometimes blown off course and then carried away by a strong current to a land far to the east.

"Kuroshio," he said. "Kuroshio current."

This strong current, he went on, capturing one's boat would carry it steadily towards the strange land to the east, with its giant mountains, the world's largest fish; some as long as their fishing boat. Some had returned apparently, to tell tales of wondrous things; fish, people, trees, waterfalls, mountains.

They had never been out so far before and the day had suddenly turned bright and sunny, with the sea calm and almost unusually still. After an hour or so fishing, with the nets full of fewer but much larger fish, Ichiro threw in his net one final time.

"Uwa!" he shouted as a huge splash and then a great commotion took place before him. Struggling with the net, he called for Akihito's help and soon they had pulled in a tremendous fish. Both laughed in unison and Ichiro could see his fishing mentor was very proud!

Excitement grew as they reached the dock and Akihito held up the heavy fish in both hands and shouted, "Ichiro!" A cheer went up from the four or five fishermen gathered near the dock. Ichiro's heart sang, as he envisioned returning home with the large fish amid praise from the beaming Akihito. Yet it was not to be and this day would be the saddest of his young life.

Akihito had soon recognized that while Ichiro loved to go out on the boat and had become an excellent fisherman, Dashiro was not so inclined. More and more often he was given other duties; repairing the roof when the rains came in, turning up the garden bed for planting the daikon and other vegetables.

Dashiro could now replace a broken chair leg, a rotting door frame and even earned small sums by helping neighbours with such chores. This, however, gave him much more time with the flirtatious Myumi. Ichiro now harboured a suspicion that perhaps the special times with Myumi were happening with Dashiro also, by looks the other two exchanged when they thought no one was looking. But, surreptitiously, Ichiro was always looking!

In the early days of their time with the family, Dashiro had become bored, strained by lack of excitement, and more and more went to the village for routine visits. Often he had tried to talk Ichiro into leaving the family for a life in the village or better still, in one of the other fishing villages which lie along the coast.

They would occasionally see these small encampments when far out at sea, and had once or twice met boats from another of these villages. But Ichiro, who had never in his remembered life had a real family; been part of a laughing, loving family with both parents and siblings, was loathe to leave.

But this day, it would all come to an end. The two fishermen returned home with the exciting news of Ichiro's catch to find the other three beaming with joy and excitement. Katsumi could not contain her joy!

"Married!" Katsumi shouted.

"They are going to be married!"

Dashiro and Myumi beamed at them; smiling at each other and with Dashiro's arm against Myumi's shoulder. Ichiro did not know what to do or say and so stood in stunned silence. The flirtatious looks and behavior of Myumi towards him; the secret smiles and even a rare brush of his arm with her hand and the secret, forbidden kisses had somehow led Ichiro to believe that he was the chosen one.

Saki was brought out for this festive occasion; the first such fermented drink Ichiro had enjoyed, although he knew Dashiro had secretly imbibed with his older village friends. Soon, he too felt giddy and lightheaded and the evening was passed in light-hearted laughter and banter.

But the next morning, Ichiro awoke with a heavy heart and did not know how he could carry on in this household with the two lovebirds. Thus, he was glad to rush off to the boat and spend the day alone at sea; a privilege that Akihito had recently granted him. Ichiro made sure he did not look at Myumi and felt only a dull anger at her, as he felt she had been playing with his feelings.

Things now changed in the small household, as preparations were being made for the coming ceremony in which Dashiro and Myumi would become husband and wife. More and more Ichiro would escape to the loneliness of the boat, sullenly bring home the catch, while both Akihito and Katsumi made sure to give him extra attention and affection, sensing his sadness.

One day, alone out on the bay, he ventured farther out than

ever before, again looking for that elusive large catch. The calm waters suddenly began to heave and toss and the small boat plunged about in rough waters. A loud booming sound reached his ears and he looked fearfully towards the shore, now far away.

Ichiro had not yet spent a lifetime on the waters, like Akihito and some of the others, but had heard tales of boats suddenly hit by heavy seas and high winds. Once, they said, four fishing boats gathered together over a run of sea bass. All four boats had ended up many, many miles apart on different areas of the coastline after a storm.

Yet, this was the strangest storm Ichiro had ever encountered. As he looked quickly towards shore to make sure he was headed in the right direction, he could see trees weaving and shaking, yet there was no wind. The buildings he could see were looking strange, as though they were being shuffled about by a large hand, as indeed they were.

Was it the land rocking? Or was it his small boat?

Huge waves now moved the boat twenty or thirty feet upwards, then a sudden plunge down. Ichiro hung on to the mast in terror. Then another wave and he saw the shoreline in his vision disappear under that wave in a hallucination he must have invented.

Suddenly, the boat lurched aside and Ichiro's head hit the deck with a bang! It was the last he knew.

Part Two

THE SEA

Chapter Eight

Ichiro awoke. The first thing he saw was a splash of dried blood where his head must have crashed against the decking. He felt his head now, which hurt almost beyond endurance, and his hand when he looked was covered in blood.

Was this a dream?

A nightmare?

A bright sun scalded his hot face and the sea was calm. Ichiro had no idea how long he had been unconscious or perhaps asleep. The boat was drifting on a calm sea.

He reached for his water. His mouth was dry and only thirst remained to him, along with the still throbbing pain in his head. He drank ravenously to assuage his rampant thirst, but as he looked all around that silent sea and saw no land, he knew instinctively he must save his water.

Suddenly, as he turned to rise, his hand barely missed a gelatinous mass on the deck near him. There lie a stinging jelly fish which Ichiro had learned the hard way during his recent apprenticeship as a fisherman, would cover anything it touched with a stinging coat of jelly.

On a shallow wave some debris floated by; parts of a broken branch with green leaves still attached, bits of flotsam, a length of fishnet still bobbing along, held aloft by its float. Out of habit, he felt for the wind and it was just a rather light breeze. Ichiro had no idea which way to go, or even if his torn sail would return him to shore.

Rummaging through every foot of the boat, he retrieved the

long fish knife they worked with and dug through the cotton bag he always carried. Ichiro found his abacus, which he often brought along just to practice with and this always seemed to please Akihito, especially when Ichiro asked for his help and advice. There was his father's tanto! He would surely need it! He also found an old shirt and a small pouch of seeds to chew on. But, there was nothing in the bag that would save a life or even prolong it!

He drifted slowly for hours, in and out of sleep with the slow rocking of the waves. Once, he threw a scrap of wood overboard that had been knocked from the railing but it sailed nowhere, just lie quietly on the water. No land was in sight throughout that long day but Ichiro hoped, wished, that perhaps the morning would bring that longed for sight of land. Then it was night.

Again he woke to a brilliant blue sky, the skin on his cheek hot and dry; stinging where the burning sun was beating down on it, unprotected. Out to sea, a different scene appeared before him. Today, a long quiet swell, covered with little white crests. Again, there was no land in sight, only the slow lap-lapping of the waves; the silent sea.

His small craft bobbed up and down in a rhythmic dance that soon grew maddening in its endless regularity. Looking overboard, there was no flotsam or sign of land nearby and Ichiro started! A strange fish passed alongside his boat. Large and grey, it was of a type he had not seen before, but then his experience out in deep ocean was limited. Another day passed.

This day however, was a day of work. What to eat? As he began to recover from his aching head, Ichiro's appetite returned to its youthful vigor.

"I will soon starve," he thought. "I must eat!"

Ichiro's glance fell automatically to the deck where his last catch of fish was entwined in its pile of netting.

"Yes!" he exclaimed to himself and reached for the slimy, grey mass.

Those long, boring, never-ending days of sitting with the fish; cleaning, scaling, then hanging and drying them now became his salvation.

Ichiro retrieved his wide-brimmed straw hat from where it lie on the deck and sat quietly all of that morning and into the afternoon doing what he had done so many times before and finally, his thankfully large catch was hanging to dry in the hot sun on lines he rigged from his nets and ropes.

"Enough!" he exclaimed aloud. Yes, there would be enough for many, many days. The problem now would be water, as his meagre supply would be soon exhausted, even with his careful and infrequent tiny sips.

As he awoke the next morning, Ichiro shouted with excitement. From the first moment he realized he was adrift at sea, he knew his greatest challenge would be lack of water. Stories and tales spun by the older fishermen reminded Ichiro that getting hung up on a slack tide or staying out too long during an exceptional day's catch could result in thirst.

"Yes!" he shouted again. Somehow in this silent and scary world of isolation it seemed even his own voice brought solace.

This day, the sea was covered in a thick mist and he would soon learn more of that same sea. Always and forever the only thing he could rely upon was its ever-changing nature.

On this morning as he looked ahead, Ichiro's eyes fell on the stack of cotton sail that lie crumpled and torn on the deck. In a crease and narrow fold of the sail a small pocket had formed and it was now full of water.

"What!" Had it rained in the night and he hadn't felt it?

He tasted it hesitantly. Not salt -- it was fresh water. Not rain, he realized. It was just the dew which had gathered during that long night. The heavy mist had fallen and everything on deck was soaking with dew.

Many times during those long nights he would awaken.

Sometimes to driving clouds, often to a heaving moonlit sea.

Other times dreaming dreams of forgotten childhood scenes.

Still other times the dreaded hours of sitting in the zendo -- wishing for sleep but afraid of the sharp pain as the stick fell on his thin shoulders.

Ichiro never knew just how long the night was in his young life.

Or how brilliant the stars were on a calm and clear night.

Or how the moon changed hour to hour with clouds drifting by in a rising breeze.

"I will not be afraid!" Ichiro's voice was loud and forceful. "Yes! I am a good fisher!"

Talking to himself to relieve the silence, the boredom, and sometimes the fear and panic became his new habit. Strangely enough, although Ichiro had begun his lonely conversations with himself just to hear a human voice, he found this began to buoy his spirits! At times of deep loneliness or fear, he would shout loudly, words of encouragement.

"Yes! I will soon find land!" And he would believe it.

But now, there was water.

That first morning, his instinct had been to lean over the deck railing and splash a handful of cool water on his burning and bloodied face. With a howl he realized the salt was more powerful than his need for cool comfort. He knew also, as a trained fisherman that the first rule taught him was to never,

ever drink of that plenitude of cool water; no matter how hot the day, or how long. No matter that water stores were low or even gone. And this thirst could be deadly. Three weeks without much food was the folklore, but only three days without water and those in great discomfort; then true suffering, then death.

Now, Ichiro had the answer.

That evening, he formed his torn sail into a land of hills, mountains and deep ravines. Just as he'd hoped and prayed, the next morning those shallow lakes and ravines he had formed were full of water. Enough to last the day if he cautiously doled it out to himself in small, steady streams. Now, Ichiro could possibly live until land came in sight or better still, he was rescued by the other fishermen when he did not return from the day's work.

The custom had always been if a friend or fellow fisher did not return that day and did not drift in on the late tides, the others would go out in the morning to find him. This was especially important if a storm had suddenly come up, leaving no time to head for shore before the huge waves came.

Ever hopeful, trying every moment to believe this would happen, Ichiro also knew that his last glimpse of the village being rocked and torn under what he now knew was an epic earthquake of a fierce power he had never seen or felt before, that rescue from the village would not come.

The dark omen of the oarfish had been correct.

"One. Two. Three."

Ichiro counted aloud as he took his knife, used only for cleaning fish to keep it sharp and scored three shallow gashes on his damaged mast. When one future day, he would count the many marks he had made and they were fifteen, he knew rescue would never come.

Chapter Nine

On and on he drifted. One day like another, but not.

The hunger in his gut; the same. The sun searing his exposed skin, the constant licking his lips, as though he might find moisture there, or solace. The constant lap-lapping of the waves, now soft, now louder as the winds changed: the same.

Yet each day's drama unfolded anew.

A startling journey into the past, where strict and disciplined head monks would order hours of sitting or kneeling meditation in the temple. Skies burst with winter rains and one rushed to gather wooden buckets and bowls to catch the deluge now dripping, pouring through the old split-shingled roof before all bedding and carpets were hopelessly drenched. Floors creaked with cold in the rare snows that would blanket the temple buildings and hid them from view until one almost stepped into a dark wall.

Or, a small village appeared suddenly before his startled eyes. A village where he lived with a close and large family; brothers, sisters, parents, various aunts and uncles, cousins, and grandparents. A never-ending procession of chats, encounters, hugs, arguments and meals. Loved and belonging. Kind and unkind moments, as he shoved against someone's belongings, or beliefs, and was screamed at in rage. Or rescued a sister's cat from a neighbour's dog and received a warm hug.

Each day a procession of aliveness, motion, voices, moments.

Some days, Ichiro feared he would go mad. He might wake from a deep slumber to hissing waves and find himself in terror at the unknown demons and wrathful deities which populated his dreams and nightmares.

Other times, awake in the boat; sitting, sitting, staring off into the endless waves, he could feel he was going mad; drifting slowly towards madness with the enemy now known. It was himself.

At these times, Ichiro felt that one day he would suddenly and violently fling himself into that same placid, unending ocean and bring an end to his fear, his loneliness, his torture. During one of these times; those times Ichiro was weary with fear, exhausted from keeping awake and keeping the small sail either furled or unfurled, anger and rage of the treatment by his vapid and unfaithful sweetheart, he decided he could not take it anymore.

"Tattaima!"

"Now!" he shouted.

With one foot up on the rail, he grabbed it with his hand and began to lift himself up and over. Suddenly, just as quickly as the desire to end his life had struck him, it was gone.

But in that moment of insanity, Ichiro had seen his body sink beneath the waves and the little boat plunge forward with no one on board. Would his lifeless body slowly, slowly drift downwards and sink to the bottom only to be rapidly engulfed by hundreds of small crab-like creatures?

Or would he float aimlessly about for days or weeks; drying, dehydrating in the hot sun and drifting perpetually like a dead, dried tree limb with birds pecking out his eyes; sitting on his exposed chest.

Then in an instant, he awoke to the present moment.

"Gomen'nasai! Gomen'nasai!" Again, Ichiro shouted only to himself. "I am sorry!"

Ichiro could not believe it had come to this: could not believe the depth of his cowardice, his lack of courage and fortitude. Where had his resolve gone? The gift of strength from generations of Samurai forefathers? What had happened to the depth of his knowledge of life, of death he had learned of; no experienced in those hundreds of hours upon the mat?

"Yurushi." I forgive.

Just as suddenly as the temptation had come, Ichiro had forgiven his juvenile self. Felt for a moment were the hardships he had been through; the loss of family, the discipline of the zendo, too much for a mere boy. Then the harsh reality of being swept out to sea, the loneliness, the uncertainty each day brought whether he would live or die: he forgave it all.

Ichiro breathed deeply. He breathed in salt air. He breathed out sadness and fear. He breathed in peace and forgiveness. He bent to retrieve a piece of dried tuna where it was stored in his reed basket. He sat, ate to fullness and then slept.

Days passed, one day like another. Once, a great blue shark rubbed against the side of his craft, plunging him into the now familiar state of panic, then it swam slowly off into the distance; its fin just appearing in random bursts in that vast sea. Looking overboard as he often did, just to distract himself from the constant anxiety over his predicament or to relieve his boredom, he spied a huge shoal of sardines, larger than any he had ever seen. Was he nearing land?

Perhaps a week or two had passed when one very fine day with a brilliant blue sky, a sudden wind came up. As the morning hours passed, the wind increased and stirred the ocean up finally into a roaring sea. Flying spray, crashing waves; the sea had turned to chaos and suddenly the now constant boredom and anxiety over his fate was conquered by even greater chaos in Ichiro's heart.

The roaring seas rolled ever closer towards him and he could not now tell if it was the winds or a sudden change in the current. What relief he felt as the first huge wave came towards him and in the midst of his white-knuckled terror as he held the rails, his trusty craft rose up into the wave: higher and higher. Just as Ichiro felt he had breathed his last, the small boat rose up, up and over.

Just as smoothly, it slid down into the trough of the next great wave and up again! Finally, close to dusk the wind died down but he could not tell if he was still heading east or now westerly. A huge phosphorescent squid flopped onto the deck and Ichiro just laughed. It seemed another omen, this time of good luck and in his joy at having conquered the storm, his first alone at sea, he picked up the giant creature and flung it back into the waves.

For the first time Ichiro encountered many beings up close like the squid on this journey to nowhere that were once just stories told aboard the small boat, sitting around on the docks with the other fishers, or just over a bowl of rice at dinner. Like the oarfish, the legends of strange and wonderful creatures one would encounter at sea were now a reality.

The water had slowly changed somehow into a deep vibrant green and Ichiro could feel a new cold had been swept into it. Days of cool, clear calm followed his first storm at sea and now Ichiro's past came into play. Perhaps it was a small feeling of triumph that he had conquered something; something strange and nebulous, and not only the sea, but something within himself.

As the days passed, his own past came more and more into play. Instead of the fear and anxiety of the sea and its storms, winds and waves; instead of the paralyzing boredom he had only recently endured, there was something new. For the first time, he returned to a moment of peace and then he was reliving a part of his past he had never deemed important: the hours, days, weeks and months of discipline sitting on his mat.

Now, he sat again. The deck of the boat his mat, where now he folded up his torn sail to take away the hardness of the old wooden deck, and just... sat.

No thought. No fear. Just a deep breath. Then another. His thoughts calm, gone even in the constant lap, lap of the never-ending but now friendly, gentle waves.

On his most optimistic days, Ichiro could believe that he would soon strike land, even though it might not be his own village. And he knew now that he would have the fortitude to explore that wishful land, to trek up or down its shores in search of a home; a people who would take him into their hearts and homes.

It seemed now that he had lost his fear of the vast ocean which had become his master. Ichiro began to notice that each day there were subtle changes in the sea. He had become accustomed to the almost daily small flying fish that landed on his deck and they soon became a staple of his diet though not ever considered gourmet food by the fishermen he knew.

"Yes!" Again he shouted in rapture when one day, with a sudden inspiration he grabbed the biggest of the flying fish on his deck and used it as bait to enhance his fishing line. To his great delight, he had indeed caught something, and then amazement when he realized he had hooked a twenty pound dolphin which fed him for a week, and longer when he dried the remainder.

Occasionally, memories of Myumi would erase the knowledge that she now belonged to Dashiro and fill his heart with joy at the warmth, affection and love he had experienced in her soft, white arms.

Somewhere, he knew that this challenging, life-altering

experience of being lost at sea had formed his heart into that of a man. That he was strong and able and that somewhere on that shore of fantasy and desire he would one day reach a young woman with bright dark eyes to take his hand and lead him into her heart and home. That he would have a shack for his nets and a small but sturdy boat. That small children would arrive, with many strong sons; he and his love would give them strong names.

"Katsuo!"

"Jirokichi!"

"Kiyotaka!"

Chapter Ten

One evening, amidst his constant dreams and fantasies, for this was all that now kept him from madness, Ichiro felt with unshakable and unwavering certainty that this was not a dream or wishful thinking; that it was a definite foreknowledge of the path his future life would take.

With renewed optimism, he again began to mark out the continuity of his days, carving the five or six he had neglected to mark into the old but solid wood of his mast. He could not have known that all of sixty-three dashes would mark the end of his journey.

By now, his skin had become a deep, dark brown and often as he sat he could feel the sweat, saturated now with salt, running down his back.

The days were strange, uneven, and curious. One day, a warm and friendly sun would cheer his heart. Ichiro would look out on the never-ending horizon and imagine that just behind that next wave, the hills and forests of his homeland would come into view.

Next day, tumultuous waves might strike fear into his heart as the narrow craft rolled and swung in the swift winds that had come up in the night. Then, a storm so frightening that Ichiro felt his end was near as waves washed over the rails almost faster than he could bail out the water with his wooden bucket.

One day, he noticed that it was unusually calm; not a wave, a motion or a movement in the eerily smooth waters which surrounded him. Yet after several days of this, another weather system appeared and would last for the rest of his journey. Remembering his talk that day on the beach with Akihito with his decades of wisdom concerning that same sea, Ichiro knew he had found the great current.

"Yes!" he shouted.

"Kuroshio!" The great current!

Once captured by this benign current, went the old tales, one could just post a light sail and the soft winds would carry a boat to strange lands with no rowing or effort on the part of the fisherman. One only needed to shift the sail to take advantage of slight changes in the weather pattern.

Ichiro now dug beneath his bench, through the crevices and crannies of the boat where extra fishing nets, hooks and gear had been stowed. Amongst the gear was an old shirt which was torn and then repaired, torn and repaired again until it was relegated as rags for wiping hands while at work on the boat.

Over the next two days and with many hours of work, Ichiro somehow managed to repair his torn sail, attach it to the cracked and slightly damaged mast and watch as this new and slightly gentle breeze began to fill out his handiwork. Now, his sail moved him along at several times the speed he had been drifting. His heart sang; his hopes rose now he had at least a small degree of power and control over this strange new life he had unwillingly entered.

Some days, just to relieve his boredom; brought by the mind-dulling deadness of the sea, the sky, the limited expanse of the small craft, Ichiro would throw out a line and hook into the sea. First one, then another type of hook, hoping for something to strike or for the minutes to pass. Then, a strike!

"Yes!" Something had jerked the line and it was too far out now to be seaweed. Ichiro pulled and pulled, and finally pulled up a fish which he had never before encountered. Was it good to eat? He would find out!

"Seiko!" Success! After cleaning it, saving the scraps for more bait and drying the strangely dark fish in the hot afternoon sun, it became a tasty morsel for his dinner. Ichiro was to find, using his line and hook; sometimes his net, that there were strange and unusual fish in these waters.

Once, a school of porpoises, a score or more fled past; too many to count! And the flying fish were everywhere. They sprang up here and there, Ichiro watched them fly up, glitter for a moment in the sun, then dive beneath the surface to vanish. Besides the familiar species like sardines, he once saw a large fish at dusk that flashed with brilliant phosphorescence. Another time, Ichiro gasped in fright as a large fish which looked like the eel fish, only with arms or wings, looked as though it might climb into the boat. Then, something he could only describe as a sea monster rose up beside him, its dark black eye looked towards him, then vanished as the monster sank beneath the waves.

One day, as Ichiro sat absentmindedly sorting through his nets, baskets, and the assorted fishing gear normally stuck under the decks and benches, he came again upon his abacus. A thought; a vague memory of counting, counting flashed. His father, Katsumasa, sitting with the abacus and sliding beads back and forth, back and forth to teach a young, uninterested boy its secrets. Then, in the kitchen with Masato, counting, counting endless cups of rice and barley. Now, a sudden inspiration! Ichiro played with those same beads, sliding them back and forth idly as he wondered what he could count to relieve the tedium of long, long hours upon a quiet sea.

Waves? He counted. One, two. On and on until he grew so bored and distracted that the abacus fell suddenly from his hands as he slid into a sleepy daze. Yet, finally this abacus would be another ally in his fight to conquer the incessant boredom, the horrendous tedium of weeks at sea.

And one day, as the now common flights of small fish veered overhead, unto the deck, some flashing in the sun, Ichiro automatically grabbed his abacus and began to count! Faster and faster! Every drop of attention sharply focussed on the small creatures flying around him. Eventually, he lost count, then began again.

It was now a game, a contest, a competition between him and the fish to see if they could move quicker than he could slide the beads along. What fun! His heart pounded with excitement at this most delightful, frivolous pastime in weeks.

A new pastime to relieve the long hours of deadly monotony. And through the next days, Ichiro became quicker and quicker as each wave of the small fish flew by. A game between them, but, who was the winner? It mattered not, as each time this happened, a few precious moments were rescued from crushing boredom and the loneliness of his days.

With a deadly monotony, the wind and waves continued to push and pummel the boat but the steady ocean current continued to pull his boat straight, ever onward. At times, Ichiro had had to chew on raw fish for moisture. Now with infrequent but heavy rain showers he was lucky to easily maintain his water supply; a vast relief which helped to calm his receding fears. He was becoming proud of the new skills he was learning!

Dry parched lips, sore tongue and throat had warned Ichiro that something was amiss, although he had thankfully, sufficient water for his needs. He began to occasionally drink a small mouthful of seawater, realizing that there was little or no salt in his diet and soon, this had somehow solved the problem. He would find, strangely enough given his wretched state, that he could win a victory over small things; he could conquer his fears!

Chapter Eleven

One day, Ichiro breathed in deeply; a fresh salt tang in the air which became stronger as the day wore on. Something different! Anything out of the usual, whether with wind, sea, weather or sky gave fresh hope that something, anything might change! Was he nearing land? A new sea?

Two days later, the wind came up, freshened and then blew steadily. Seas ran high. Ichiro shouted with excitement as his sail began to fill and the boat moved more quickly, more surely through the waves. But as the sail filled, the boat turned to the wind and moved quickly in the wrong direction.

In this vast sea, was there a wrong direction? Ichiro struggled to right the sail, as he had felt so confident when he located the current that seemed to be taking him and his craft towards the east; towards the mythical lands he had heard about in those old stories. The sky quickly clouded over with the sea a succession of huge rollers.

Soon, the world was swallowed up by darkness and the noise of the sea became deafening. Crash! Huge waves began to rock the boat and Ichiro held on with every bit of youthful strength he possessed as the waves began to wash over him. It took all the strength he could summon from his now emaciated body to hurriedly take down his sail. This, he thought, would add some stability in the face of such horrendous movement.

Once, the stern swung up wildly and water rolled along the deck. Then, down, down he pitched into the next trough, and then another. Two or three tremendous waves followed, and then smaller waves and Ichiro prayed the worst was over. But it was not. Higher, more startling waves soon followed.

Trembling among the waves, Ichiro clung to the mast in darkness. Water poured off his hair, his hands grew cold and stiff. Every muscle was strained almost beyond endurance, but after this experience he felt only a great jubilation. He had become, finally, a seaman!!!

Next day, although the seas still ran high, the weather began to freshen. The wind had changed course. Blue upon blue; a world of blue. Ichiro now saw flying fish, the tiniest flying fish he had seen, hundreds of them it seemed. The boat still rose up and down but more slowly and calmly; up and down, up and down; a meditation. Ichiro though, did not want to go back and forth, back and forth, hither and thither relentlessly over that vast sea.

The sun began to go down and a full moon shone upon the sea. Stars came out. The stars! A world of glory. And Ichiro discovered that by turning his sail, he could follow those same stars. The same ones he had always known.

In the days to come, a strange elation overtook Ichiro; a confidence he had not felt before in his young life. He had not grown up upon the sea and when he became marooned upon it, the boat was his nemesis: an enemy that might lead to his death.

But now, the boat had become His Boat! He had conquered it! He was no longer afraid and knew with a stout heart that he would never be. Ichiro had touched within himself a depth of strength and courage that would be with him for life and although he could not yet know this with certainty, he felt it; knew it in his bones. Ichiro had been tested to his limits and with this new maturity, other events in his young life became clearer. His fear had turned to elation, each memory of forgotten days came with a new clarity.

When Myumi now entered his thoughts and memories as

had happened daily in recent weeks, a new and amazing experience took place. Ichiro began to see Myumi as the immature, silly creature she had been. He could see that she had been playing flirtatious games with both he and Dashiro. He recalled that it had been just a day or two before the marriage was announced that he and Myumi had shared their most passionate encounter yet, with his caresses more bold and her body pressing back in a breathless Yes! This day, instead of a broken heart, Ichiro felt grateful, almost happy that he had been rescued from a lifetime with this fickle and shallow young woman. He would never have wished this kind of female to become the mother of his children; to feed, teach, heal and raise them.

In the following days, a new calm came into his heart. A new calm had also come unto the clear sea that now rolled beneath him in constant slow rolling waves. It had seemed weeks since the great storm and when Ichiro checked the marks on his mast one day, it had been twenty-two days. Sitting, sitting, watching the cool green sea pass before him. Grabbing a flying fish as one landed on the deck, before it could flop off and over, now took up just a small bit of his time. Although he had not a lot to eat, Ichiro now had sufficient for his needs and there was almost no movement in his days. Collecting water from his arrangement of old bits of torn sail, sometimes an old shirt or his bucket, became second nature. He had devised so many ways of satisfying his thirst that drinking water was no longer a problem. To cleanse and freshen his often sweaty body, he had learned how to slowly lower himself from the side of the boat. He learned how to hold on just enough to keep from loosening his grip as he slipped his face in the clear sea that he lived with; that had become his universe.

Days of calm filled the weeks that passed. A day came when Ichiro almost wished for a horrific storm that might drive him into fear, or even terror or panic just to relieve the unending boredom of being alone in the world with just his thoughts and that calm, calm, flat sea.

His mind now had an eternity to bring up from the depths of his being, his earliest childhood days. His father Katsumasa; stern but loved who had one day vanished forever. His mother Tsuya; warm, caring, always beside him. Visions of her holding the young Ichiro filled his heart with warmth: he had been deeply loved.

Ichiro's time as an orphan now moved through his being and became altered as it; time, Ichiro and the boat moved along. He remembered old Kiku, how she had taken him in; become his missing mother. His boyhood friends and now, he remembered not the insecurity of no home and family but the memories of those childhood games they had all played. Ichiro realized he was not, nor had been, a lonely and unwanted orphan but that an entire village of neighbours, friends and distant relatives had cared for and about him. And finally, old Chogun, Masato and the monks had taken him in and guided him towards becoming a brave and happy youth.

In these weeks at sea, the days had changed him from a lost, unhappy soul into a strong and valiant warrior. At first, the ocean was his enemy with its terrifying waves, its unpredictable nature, its fierce winds. Yet now, it had become his friend and mentor, leading him from that unhappy life into a new one where he had conquered not only those tremendous waves, but his fear, his angst.

A new and different Ichiro now sat on the deck of his beloved small craft and his time in the zendo became his salvation. He sat. Just sat. Hands on knees, eyes half closed looking towards the horizon but not focused on anything. His mind quiet. He sat.

Those long hours of practice now gave him his rewards. He

began once again, to practice. Instead of insane monotony, now he saw his time sitting on the deck, nets piled up for a cushion, as his way to enlightenment; to knowledge, to wisdom, to life. A new life. He sat.

Ichiro found with the change in his mind, his memories; a change came also in the world around him. Strange things began to happen in his mind as he continued to sit. Startled, Ichiro one day realized he could see into the future. He saw himself standing in a forest, looking upwards where a strange bird croaked out a warning, or was it a strange welcome?

Another time, staring out to the endless sea, he saw before him in the distance a familiar village; then the mountain he had seen break apart and tumble into the sea. Would he someday return to that world?

And then a storm so devastating it would test his every resolve.

Chapter Twelve

Ichiro awoke finally to a sea that had changed. The weeks of sitting, sitting, waiting for something to happen were now over.

The sea that day was strange; patterns of wind and waves Ichiro had not experienced before. That strange sea was running in long even ridges, not high and wild like in previous storms, but steadily increasing in height and depth. As the day wore on and turned to dusk, then night, the rhythmic rocking and slow rise and fall of the boat got the better of him. Half dazed, he fell asleep.

With a sudden start, Ichiro woke! He was being hurled around and sideways. Water poured over him. The sea; chaos, like his thoughts.

Huge waves, then smaller ones. There was no pattern or sense to what was happening; where the wind was coming from, which way it was blowing. He pitched and rolled.

Torrents of sea sickness, the likes of which he had never experienced grabbed at his insides like the claw of some great hawk and everything he had ingested, eaten or drank for days it seemed, now came hurtling from his mouth to cover his arms and legs, his clothing, the sail and decking.

The waves came hissing along, the sea danced around him. Everything moved. Boards creaked and groaned. On these windy, rain-lashed nights, Ichiro would pull his sail down and run with bare poles. Now, standing to restrain his small sail and tie it to the mast, Ichiro was almost thrown overboard and in this terrifying sea, would have spelled his end.

After what seemed a lifetime of this, but might have been a day, or inconceivably maybe only hours, he felt a slight change in the waves; a break in the constant plunging and flinging madness. When morning came, the sea was bright and calm.

The waves rose high, then down, massive waves but calmer now. The water seemed to have changed from the deep green of the last weeks to a more subtle but brilliant blue. This day was quiet but even here, far out at sea Ichiro sailed past the floating feather of a bird, a white bird. The first he had seen since the current had taken him east weeks ago.

Next day he woke up to find a common sight, but now with an unusual and startling quality. One of the usual flying fish that had landed but hadn't yet managed to leap overboard was being attacked and devoured by dozens of the smallest crabs he had ever seen!

In days to come it seemed Ichiro had entered a new world, as indeed he had. One day, he encountered an immense mass of plankton, which had seemingly floated from somewhere. The seas were too deep here, he thought, for it to be normal. The next time a huge wave hit, plankton blew, flew on board and it was everywhere.

Ichiro began to gather enough to eat. Perhaps if he dried it on his lines, he could add it to his daily fare for a welcome change to the diet of dried fish he had endured for weeks and weeks.

Now, each day might bring something new and Ichiro was becoming surprised at nothing. Thus, when the day came and he awoke to several sharks, very large sharks circling his boat, instead of the fear and panic he might once have felt, he was only calmly amused. Would they follow him forever? And one day as he dipped down with his bucket for water to clean fish, would sharp teeth grab and hold him? Pull him down into obscurity? Into hell?

Ichiro laughed as his nets pulled aboard the smallest shark he could ever have imagined. He had tempted it with some bait and now it lie flapping over the deck in wild abandon. Ichiro caught it by its tail, making sure to keep well away from its jaws; sharp and scary for such a small specimen.

No, he would not eat it, he decided, no matter how hungry he might be. However, it did make a tempting bit of bait for the next catch, a nice-sized tuna which swallowed most of the small shark and then itself became dinner for Ichiro.

Only once on this whole voyage did Ichiro see a rare snake mackerel, which he recognized from a day fishing with Akihito. The older fisher had been excited about the catch, telling Ichiro just how seldom this fish was seen, let alone caught. Soon, it was cold and wet, flapping on the deck. A treat for dinner.

These days it seemed, Ichiro was never without the company of birds. One day, looking out dejectedly at a sea and sky of fine drizzle, a solitary albatross went by, flying so closely to the boat it must have been as curious about Ichiro as he was by the rare bird.

Tiny petrels had come one night and spent it squawking, keeping him awake almost until dawn and they had spent the next day squawking and flitting in the foam. So plentiful and playful were they, a smile came to Ichiro's lips and a decision to not capture one or two in his net and have them for the next day's meal.

Squid passed, shoals of them and Ichiro managed to capture a net full. Yet, they were the tiniest squid he could have imagined; some the size of a finger! As the days passed, each one revealing something new, Ichiro awoke more and more excited to see what the day would bring.

Seaweed began to grow on his boat, which since the storm had been slowly, slowly drifting to the east. The stars seemed to be stationary now in their assigned places in the hierarchy of the sky. Until the storm it had seemed the sky, sun, moon and stars rotated in a chaotic frenzy across the sky.

Then, a day came to mark the definite beginning in this new world. Away in the distance, a plume of water reached for the sky. Not wind; not waves.

"Yes!"

"Yes!" A whale. Ichiro had only rarely seen them from a distance in the secluded bays and harbours of the village, but had heard more folklore, tales and stories of other fishers who had encountered these giant behemoths of the sea.

The spray shot up, closer and closer now and Ichiro could see it was not only one. The whales came nearer and nearer and his heart almost stopped! He felt a strange sensation new to him; a combination of happiness, excitement, fear and fun!

"Uwa!" he shouted aloud.

"Uwa!"

The whales drew nearer and nearer until finally one actually dove beneath his boat! Ichiro held his breath but the whale just seemed to be playing. It surfaced nearby, then slowly, along with the others, swam out of sight.

Then, a calm sunny day with pleasant light winds and Ichiro spent most of it checking his sail and repairing any small tears and made some minor repairs also to the rigging. Then birds came, some familiar; puffins in large flocks. Then strange small birds that he had never seen before, large drifts of them.

And fish, zebra fish that he had seen before. Next, for many days a strange mist enveloped the boat. Then fog, which grew thicker. Soon, a different mix of fog; deeper, denser fog, then softening to a thin mist, then fog again. Now Ichiro had no idea of where he might be? On the sea? On his way through a deep and wide river somewhere between cliffs? It was all a dream!

Ichiro awoke next morning to white spray crashing! Large broad waves moved him along. Waves? These had become commonplace for him... yet?? This day, something was different!

"Hold on!"

His boat was drifting inexorably towards a white wall of crashing waves. Then, the dull thud of surf! He was lifted up in the air. Later, Ichiro's only memory of this was tumbling forward, then down he sank.

Somewhere, a vision of high white snow-capped mountains flashed before him, but was it a dream, a memory or a living picture of the scene before him? As quickly as it had come, it disappeared into mist, clouds and fog.

"Hold on!" Ichiro shouted to himself.

Waves came rolling in long lines. Ichiro saw rocks! Sandy beaches? It was growing dark but sandy white beaches, like those of his homeland were surely there in the mist. Had he rotated somewhere in a dream that he could not remember and returned to his homeland?

Then, the small boat hit the shore with a crash and stayed there; lodged between great rocks which stood like sentinels on the beach. The boat was damaged slightly but still intact; a testimony to the expert craftsmen in that faraway village. Ichiro stood for a long while in shock and disbelief. How long, he did not know. Then he stepped ashore.

Ichiro stood in ankle-deep water, shallow waves lapping at his feet. He stood on sand. Rocks nearby. Night coming on.

A young lad had stepped onto the Kaza Maru.

A young man stepped off and into a strange new world.

Chapter Thirteen

It was the night of the full moon. Ichiro stood quietly, calmly, and looked at his surroundings. Before him the sea; now his friend so familiar had it become. Behind him, the land with its dense, dark forest represented the unknown. Looking north, the beach continuing in both an unbroken line of white sand backdropped by forest and broken rock tumbled down from the mountains. Looking south, more white sand and rock; but a curve taking away from his line of vision the drama of crashing waves, windswept rock, and forest.

Where to go? Back into his boat? The known? The familiar? Safety? No. It was time to sleep. Ichiro suddenly felt the tension in his body, the tired and exhausted arms and legs, his whole being suffused with only a desire to rest.

A deep breath, then a sudden determination and Ichiro walked towards his boat and pulled hesitantly on its prow. Nothing moved. He pulled again and felt a slight movement where it slid against the sand beneath. Another deep breath and this time, with all his strength, every bit of power and determination he could build from within, one long and final heave.

"Yes!" he called aloud to no one. To the moon, the tides, the silent guardians of the forest. The boat moved tentatively several feet in his direction.

"I did it!"

Now the challenge before him grew easy. Ichiro pulled, strained and dug his feet into the sand feeling his friend Kaza

Maru begin to glide more and more easily. Up, up towards the towering trees and finally, a hundred feet or more beyond the line of the surf, he made a final effort and the boat headed into a cleft between two rocks which lie at the edge of the forest.

Ichiro climbed in, away from the roaring, crashing surf. Searching through the debris of tattered sail, old rags and fish netting, he clustered together a pile soft and large enough to sleep upon. He lay down, nestled his head into a comforting hollow and slept.

Dawn broke. Although the sun was invisible behind the forest, Ichiro could see the smooth, calm waves far out at sea glistening in the morning sun. He rose, stretched and at once, felt the sharp pangs of hunger within. Digging through nets, sticks, buckets and baskets on the boat, he found enough dried seaweed and fish to calm his angry stomach.

Food. Water. These were not only first on his mind from the weeks of wandering hopelessly lost at sea, but the demands of his being that had been with him since he lost his home. Now he knew, food and water he must find, and soon. Walking along the beach in the shady place between sand and sea he looked, smelled, then shouted!

"Hamaguri!"

"I eat!" Ichiro shouted with abandon. "I eat!"

Yes, the beach was littered with clams and he gathered a handful, enough for a meal. Now water. Walking south for an hour or more, Ichiro rounded the curve of land and saw just a continuation of sand, rocks, beach and forest. Slowly he walked along, looking closely at the rich line of clams, oysters and also some other sea life he did not even recognize. Once or twice, he came upon a dead fish entangled in seaweed that had washed in on the high tides. The two-foot long fish was not familiar to him.

Still he walked, gaining hope as he perceived the rich

abundance of food along his path. Then, a soft noise from the forest behind him. Then a gurgle; a trickle of water coming from deep in the trees. He walked into the woods, following a thin stream of water as it ran crazily around trees, huge trees of a size and height he had never seen in his far-off homeland.

"Yes!" he cheered! "I will drink!"

Beneath the trees was a garden of impossible delusions! Strange-looking plants and herbs. A small flower peeking here and there, white and lovely in the soft morning light. A spiked-looking thing, a foot or so high. Ichiro picked one and began to cautiously chew. He had learned in childhood from old Kiku that not all things which grew in the woods could be eaten: that indeed, some could make one very ill. This strange, spiked herb bit savagely on his tongue and he quickly spit it out. Soon though, the biting turned into a pleasant tingling and he relished the taste.

"No!" he thought. He must be careful so he would not become ill or die from eating the local flora.

Then, at his feet a dark cluster of some berry. He picked one or two. "Delicious!" he cried, and ate them all. Ichiro followed with his hand the trailing vine which led down to the ground, then to many more vines hidden in the grasses and bush lining the stream. Ichiro happily sang as he ate handful after handful of the rich, dark purple berries, shoving them into his mouth as fast as he could pick them.

"Yes!" he cried happily. "Sweet!"

Then suddenly, a high croak before him and fluttering as a bird he had not seen before left the undergrowth and flew away into the forest. A bird meant a nest somewhere. A nest meant eggs to eat and perhaps the bird, also. After his life of dearth and want on the boat, this land appeared to present a veritable feast.

Back, back along the beach he walked, slowly now and

taking in everything he saw in this new land.

"Yes!" Ichiro had come to a momentous decision. Here, on this new land with its abundance of sea life to eat, a rich garden of herbs in the forest, birds in the air and rich, sweet juicy berries to feast upon, he would find a new life.

Ichiro was excited to finally strike land, especially one so benevolent. Yet, striking out to explore this new land was frightening and he spent days adapting to his new environment. Should he travel north along the endless beaches? North usually meant colder, windier, and more rain.

To the south, the white shell beaches beckoned and Ichiro was tempted to gather his few belongings and head that way. Yet, some unknown compulsion kept whispering in his ear to travel overland, into the heart of this new and unknown world.

"I will go!"

Ichiro felt he could not continue to stay where he had disembarked although there was food and water in plenty nearby. But, he needed more; perhaps a village with other fishermen? A mountain fastness with a hidden monastery? He had no idea where he was; whether he had journeyed for weeks only to have become turned around and now stood again in his own land? Or had he journeyed further north, where other villages were known to exist?

Struggling with his inner demons who warned Ichiro to stay put; to rest and enjoy the safety and security of his small beach, other voices told him he could not live out a life here, always alone. A journey anywhere would be filled with new sights, lands, creatures, perhaps humans.

Then, such a frightening experience that his mind was made up. He awoke the fifth morning, early as always, to the sound of snuffles and grunts. Some very large creature, no doubt. Fearfully, Ichiro raised his head slowly over the rail of the boat and spied before him the largest bear he had ever seen!

"Wao!" Never, even in old drawings, stories and tales from his homeland had such a monster even existed. Twelve feet tall? The bear was digging through the detritus that had washed up on the last tide; a collection of long strips of kelp, piles of matted seaweed, branches both large and small. Ichiro knew there would be food aplenty for as he walked along the tideline each morning he found strange fish, many crabs, both large and small and other unknown creatures.

"Grrr...!" The huge brown monster raised its hairy head. It seemed to smell something on the breeze, sniffed and then turned to look where the lad was standing. The bear gave out a mighty roar and Ichiro's heart stopped as it seemed ready to pounce. It grunted loudly, and once again. Then, it dug out and retrieved a small fish from the pile of seaweed at its feet, grunted and walked slowly down the beach with its catch until it disappeared.

Ichiro breathed out! How long had he been holding his breath? But a vision now came to him. It was the first sight of this land he'd had from the sea. The beach with its white sand and rocks. Beyond, the forest, wreathed here and there in mist and fog. Then, behind at a far distance, hovering over the low foothills were white snow-capped mountains.

"Go!" he shouted to himself. He would head off towards those mountains, hoping from those low-lying hills to get a picture of the landscape here. Were there small valleys between the hills with fields and farms? Lakes and rivers leading... somewhere? Now that his heart had calmed, the terror was gone and this would be the most exciting adventure of his young life.

But now, he must make ready.

First, he gathered from the boat anything which might be useful. His knife, drinking cup, the wisps of clothing not worn to shreds on his journey. Then, his father's tanto, the only connection with his early life. He spotted the abacus; now his friend and ally. A strange thing perhaps to take on a journey?"

"Yes!"

It could come, too. He tied everything up in a swatch of old torn netting and slung it over his back. Moving around, he decided this would not work. It was not comfortable and he would need to remove... what? Then, a sudden idea. How many times in his village had he seen farmers, old wives, passing by with their vegetables, clothing, sandals, all piled in a basket and slung over their shoulders?

Ichiro grabbed the larger of his two baskets, woven from bamboo probably decades ago. They had always been on Akihito's boat. Now, he pulled apart some netting and used the long, strong fibres to fashion a sling that would comfortably strap the basket around his back. All his belongings were neatly stashed and the basket slung over his shoulders.

"Aha!" he cried.

"It worked!" Dancing around, jumping up and down, his invention was so comfortable it was almost not there. Another success! His confidence was growing. Gone was the scared, frightened boy. He was ready for his next adventure. Ichiro now gathered seaweed, clams and small fish from the tides and spread them out on the nearby rocks where a strong sun would dry them.

Then, to work on his sandals, tightening the straps. Ichiro had gone barefoot always in the boat; no need for shoes. The fishermen always worked barefoot, so his sandals had not had any wear. They had been newly made by a villager who showed him how to care for and repair them. His feet had been growing so rapidly at the time that he had needed a new pair every few months, so these were almost not worn. They would serve him well. If needed, he could also walk barefoot through the forest as he had on his journey with Dashiro down the mountain.

Next, his knife. It had much use on his journey and he had no way to sharpen it. It was his only weapon to fight off an adversary like the bear, to gut fish, to feed himself. Ichiro knew he must guard it with his life. The tanto he would never use for practical purposes, it being almost a religious relic in his mind. With no other choice, he gathered branches from the nearest of the giant trees with his fishing knife. Although the forest floor was littered with dead branches, large and small, Ichiro felt live green branches would camouflage the Kaza Maru from sight of…. who? Anyone passing in a boat? He pushed mightily again, and this time the boat was wedged so deeply between the rocks that it was hidden from almost any direction. This took him hours but when he finished, the fish were well dried and ready to wrap in seaweed for the journey.

Now, he was ready. But the day had been long, exhausting and Ichiro was worn out. A bite of fish, a dried clam or two and it was time to sleep, although the sun had not yet set. Ichiro dreamed about running through the forest, then a growl and the bear was behind him, charging through the brush at full speed. It snarled and growled, lunged for Ichiro and he woke in a fright. But, he knew, it was just fear of the journey, the unknown that was frightening him.

He slept.

Chapter Fourteen

This morning, no golden glow of sunrise upon the water. The sea was swelling with huge waves crashing upon the shore. Wind was shaking the trees above him and whistling through the forest. But no time to waste as Ichiro picked up his basket, slung it across his shoulders, made a final check of the boat's seclusion and he was ready.

But first, thoughtfully, he stopped to make a cairn of rocks just above the tideline. Ichiro must be able to find the boat he had hidden so well. Once again, it might save his life. How to distinguish his pile of rocks from others which littered the shore?

"I am so clever!" he thought to himself. The other piles were of course, in lines, random shapes of ovals and circles. So, Ichiro's great idea was to pile the rocks in a short, sharp square. It was two feet square and a foot higher and so stood out amongst the others.

"I am so smart now!" Again, he congratulated himself on his newfound skills. Since his sojourn over the ocean he had found new thoughts, new ideas; different ideas came to him seemingly out of nowhere.

Then he turned and entered the forest. Beneath his feet, a cushion of moss of the deepest green; thick and lush in this verdant country. Some trees he recognized from his homeland such as cedars and pines but much larger here. Others he had not seen before, like a strange leafy tree with fresh young sprigs. The trunk and every branch of this tree were covered in strange grey lichen.

"Like a deer!" he shouted happily, for edges of the strange lichen did indeed stand out like that of a deer's antlers. And it lie everywhere beneath him as he walked. Startled, he stopped before another large tree; a familiar cedar but with a trunk so huge he could not have enveloped it with his arms. Looking up, its top receded into the distant sky along with the other trees in this massive forest and he could not see the top.

An hour may have passed this way, as Ichiro stopped to marvel at so many things. The forest here vastly different than that of his homeland. In what country was he now? But suddenly, as he wandered happily along, it occurred to him that he could never, ever find his way back.

Stunned, he stood there in awe at his naivety, his stupidity. What had he been thinking? Or not thinking? He was stunned at his sudden decision to just wander off into the forest. Turning around now, Ichiro realized he could not tell exactly which trees he had come through. Looking down, he could see marks where his bare feet had stepped in the soft, wet mosses, the leaves and grasses. Should he go back now, while he could? Or continue on this exciting adventure?

"No!" he shouted to no one. Again, "No!"

This exciting adventure could end only one way: with him wandering, cold, wet and starving through endless days in this vast universe of trees. Having just survived a seemingly endless ordeal at sea, Ichiro thought better of venturing further into the forest. He turned and wandered back, finding his way until he again could hear the surf crashing.

"Ho!"

The relief of reaching the beach allowed another idea to come forward. If he could again find that small creek, it would lead him upwards until he came into those high hills he had seen from shore. If lost, Ichiro could again wind his way downwards to the beach and back to his boat. Turning to his right, checking the sun for direction, he made his way south and west towards the sea.

As the rhythmic roll of the waves came closer, he finally came across what must have been the stream; narrow as it wound between rocks and the exposed roots of trees but deep here. In an hour of jumping, stepping over stone and rock he could once again see the deep ocean and soon, the beach.

"Yes!"

Ichiro shouted happily as he recognized the beach and saw his cairn standing in the distance. Now, with a more thoughtful plan he again turned, this time following the small stream as close as possible.

Suddenly, he stopped. Before him, a face so frightening he stood frozen, afraid to move. Huge eyes glared out at him, a terrifying grimace spread across its face! Not human, but a huge rock, four or five feet high and round and it would be unseen unless one wandered around it following the stream. And here, strangely, someone had carved the terrifying grin deep into the rock, perhaps warning one from entering their territory?

This frightening omen meant only one thing: men! There were others living here on this vast land, trekking the forest, climbing the mountain range. He was not alone.

Taking a deep breath, calming himself, breathing more slowly now, Ichiro continued to follow the stream and as the day wore on and the stream gaggled and gurgled among the rocks, it led him ever upwards.

Nightfall. Ichiro left the path alongside the water for safe comfort in the forest. He recalled his nights with Dashiro following the running monks those many years ago and so a night in the deep forest was not a terror but a friend. Strangely enough, there did appear to be a path up the stream.

Bears have been here, he thought, when he found the tail, fins and small bones of a fish scattered about. No fish now, but droppings here and there that showed deer also came to drink from the clean, clear mountain stream.

Wind came up as he hugged himself close to a huge trunk, partly under some smaller shrubs and bushes that grew nearby. He felt warm and safe and although Ichiro could hear the loud movement of wind in the treetops, down here below all was quiet. Nothing moved. Tired from his day's uneventful journey, Ichiro fell into a deep sleep, only interrupted when a large, strange bird squawked to herald the dawn.

"Ganbare!"

"Do your best!" he shouted to himself, to cheer himself for the day's journey and to ward off any timidity or fear that might accompany him. Ichiro gathered his gear, grabbed his basket, slung it over his shoulder and was off!

"Lots to eat!" he cheered, as the dark purple berries seemed to be everywhere the sun struck along the pathway up the streambed. Other berries, small red ones that grew close to the ground he ate sparingly to make sure they did not sicken him. He ate of the spikey herb he had tried once before and yes, it again burned his mouth and tongue horribly. But as the stinging subsided, it melted into a warm glow which stayed with him for hours.

Ichiro was learning much about this new world; what to eat, how to traverse this dramatic land. Up, up he followed the stream all that day but now it was only a thin trickle as he passed other small creeks and tributaries where they entered the main stream. But as he climbed upward, ever upward, the trees grew less dense along the pathway. The forest was beginning to thin out; the flora was changing, the grasses deeper with small wildflowers here and there.

"I am starving!" Ichiro shouted and finally stopped to eat. He dug a small bit of dried fish from his meagre store of food and chewed it slowly to make it last. Soon, he knew, he must hunt for eggs, birds or perhaps a small deer or he would indeed starve. That night, he huddled behind a large rock by the streambed as the wind became wilder and more aggressive as he climbed.

Then the dawn. An uneventful night where no hungry bear had come to devour him; no strange critter to eat his toes or fingers.

"No!" he called to no one. Again, "No!"

He was growing accustomed to the sound of his own voice; the only human noise in this vast universe of rocks and trees. His heart sank this day as the view from this height of two days travel was only deep clouds, mist and fog. A light rain came down for just a few minutes but then passed on the wind. On he went.

All that day mist and fog hid any forest, mountain or the vast sea he knew rolled away in the distance. On he trudged, startled on turning a small bend of the now diminished stream to find what seemed a fresh pile of bear scat next to the water's edge. It seemed all creatures came here to drink as he saw strange small footprints of animals he did not recognize. Up and up.

"Magic!" he called. "Wonder!"

"Amazing!"

"Funny!" Ichiro laughed at himself. During his wonderment, the clouds suddenly parted, blown away by a strong gust of wind. Before him lie an unforgettable scene. There in the far, far distance, the sea rolled and plunged; huge waves breaking on the shore but too far away to even hear them.

To the south, an unbroken line of white sand leading to a

dark, deep forest which never ended. Rising behind where he stood were undulating hills and valleys, green and lush with grasses and an occasional large rock which appeared to have tumbled down from the mountain before him. Other mountains, just as large or larger; snow-capped even in this warm weather.

"Wonder!" he called again. Even the highest peaks he had seen in his homeland were much less imposing than this behemoth of a mountain. Ichiro sat for an hour or more as the sun finally sank into that great sea to the west. All the while, visions, dreams, plans scurried through his excited thoughts as he prepared for the next stage of his adventure.

Part Three

THE ISLAND

Chapter Fifteen

Again, the dawn. Ichiro could not believe the vision which appeared before his eyes. It had not been a dream; he had not been hallucinating when he fell asleep with this vast panorama of sea, sky and mountains before him. As he looked, plotted and planned, he could see before him a way through the low foothills that lie at the foot of those impossible mountains.

"I see!" he yelled. "I see!"

Yes, there was a way. Between the great peaks, were valleys lying at a much lower elevation and he could see a pathway through them, if only he did not lose his way. Then suddenly, he gasped!

"What? What?"

Beyond the great mountains lay another vast shimmering sea. Ichiro turned again. Was he dreaming? No.

Turning now, he could see the sparkling sea in the direction he had come. A vast island? How else could one see ocean on both sides of this long slice of land. Then again, he gasped! "What... it, it cannot be?!?"

Was it really small plumes of smoke along that other far shore? Or another hallucination from chewing those astringent herbs he had foraged?

Ichiro sat for several minutes; perhaps an hour. Not thinking. Not planning. Not dreaming. Just sitting and observing as the plumes of smoke seemed to drift one way and then another in a wind or breeze. Some plumes close together; four or five in that spot. Then, it must have been miles away from the first, another plume; this one even larger. The smoke travelled upwards in a great swath only to be blown south and then dispersed by a strong wind.

This, then, is the way he must go. People. Men lighting fires with wood from the great forest. The same plumes of smoke he had seen rise from his fishing village when far out at sea on the small boat. People. Voices. He must go!

Another cairn, sturdy and square which one day might be his salvation. Then, an easy climb through grasses and wildflowers as he ascended the hill before him. Finally, he reached the top of the hill just to find another valley before him, then a steep incline up to the top of the mountain. Ichiro knew he would not take that way but turn aside into the next valley and skirt the next high mountain entirely.

When he reached the top, he began to gather stones for his next cairn. Here they were covered in moss from the constant rains and he piled them in a novel arrangement, just to amuse himself.

Would he ever return? Would this cairn ever appear on the distant horizon in the dusk, telling him that 'Yes! This was the way! You have been here before!'

Hungry, he sat to eat and now it was the last of his fish. From now on, he must forage for his daily meals. He began by eating from every small berry bush he passed on his way up the hill. Berries, he knew, would not be enough nourishment for the kind of travelling before him.

"Yes!"

Ichiro shouted again and again as he neared the summit of the hill.

"Yes!" Again, "Yes!"

But there was not the excitement in his voice there had been. Ichiro was hungry, his stomach growling for food. He was exhausted from the climb and unsure about the path forward.

After a short rest however, he again shouldered his basket and headed east across the hills towards the smoky sky. The hill led downward slightly, then up again to an even higher hill. All day it took him to reach the summit and three times he halted to build another stone cairn.

"Got it!" he shrieked.

Ichiro had managed to trap a small bird by tossing a length of netting from his basket. Now what? How to eat a small bird? But eat he must or perish! Striking its small head with a sharp stone, he then pulled the feathers from the dead bird. He cut the head off with his knife, and then hungrily chewed at it, thinking of nothing but looking off in the distance where he must travel.

Two days passed, each more exhausting than the last. Almost at the end of his strength, Ichiro made a final climb, looked down and saw below him a vast forest, leading down, down, and there in the distance the ocean plunging towards the land and those same plumes of smoke, closer now than ever.

"How to go?"

"Which way now?"

Ichiro pondered as he realized he had made his way through the mountain passes and stood now on the eastern reaches of this new land. He must reach the land of smoke and fires. There was no other choice but looking down over the large expanse of forest that lie before him, Ichiro's heart grew cold. Life was too hard!

"I cannot!" Ichiro sat looking again off into the far distance, and then fell asleep.

Waking to a sharp wind but a clear sunny day Ichiro knew he

must continue his journey, for to give up now was certain death. Each day, signs of bear appeared and once he startled one pawing through some bushes. But it only glanced at Ichiro, and then moved away. Deer were plentiful and once, a huge deer-like creature with antlers of a size he could not have imagined. Off it flew over the high meadows.

Another cairn and off Ichiro plunged into the forest. He knew he might wander off track and away from the line of smoke, yet if he kept travelling towards the morning sun he knew he would eventually reach the new coast.

Again, the cedars, fir and pine were immense; the largest and tallest trees he had ever seen. After eating several small birds, again raw, Ichiro resolved a diet of berries and herbs would have to suffice.

Another day passed. Ichiro moved through the forest like a myth; like a story that might be true, or not. As he passed, the huge column of each tree, clothed in moss, skirted with vines, underlain with fern and lichen seemed like a vision from a dream or perhaps an hallucination. In them, he lost his sense of identity. Was he human? Or just another organism, not green like the cedar boughs or grey like the lichen that caressed a branch but flesh-coloured, like a fungi that might have been there earlier, in the time of rains.

"Matsutake!" He pounced!

"I eat!" Ichiro shouted with glee. Back in memory came times wandering through the trees which surrounded the temples at his home; the walks in the forest with Dashiro filling their baskets with the delectable fungi which Masato loved to cook.

Now, he would have food, and plenty. A dozen or more very large Matsutake grew together under a stand of fir, with dozens of smaller ones nearby. Happily, Ichiro picked and picked; sliced the larger ones and wondered how many one could eat and not become ill. But, the sudden find had brought a smile to his face and he walked on along the faint pathway through the trees, singing to himself.

Then, the smile, the singing, the uplift in his spirits came to a thundering halt!

Shocked, Ichiro stood at the edge of a clearing.

"Whoosh!" Out came his breath! He did not even realize he had been holding it for many long moments as he looked in awe at the scene before him; a scene not of this earth.

The next few moments were like a dream that he had never had; a nightmare that he could never have imagined. Each tree before him had changed from a strong wooden column of green needles and rough brown appendages into a grimacing, towering and powerful enemy who was about to annihilate him.

Large eyes glowered over him; double and triple his height. Strong arms, like wings spread of an immense bird of prey hovered over him, threatening his very existence, yet strangely quiet and waiting, waiting perhaps for him to draw nearer to approach their wooden humanness in some kind of strange trap.

A fish, an eagle; monstrous parodies of the wild life he had just encountered on his flight from the raging, roaring surf. Yet, all was strange and preternaturally quiet.

All had gone still. The birds seemed to have fled the nebulous enemy who now surrounded him. His own heart whose tragic beating had slowed from its race to survive to a hollow calmness that was just as frightening in its quiet way.

Slowly, he perceived that the enemy before him had been frozen in time.

Warily, he approached the ghost-like figures, frozen in their rush towards the enemy, himself!

How long Ichiro stood in awe he could not tell. Finally, he turned away and stepped around the strange apparitions, for that they must be; he had been alone too long. Orienting himself to the sun, he stepped into the forest to continue his journey only to stop once again as it appeared a path led from the strange beings and into the trees. It seemed to stretch out before him through the woods as far as he could see and towards the same place of waves and smoke.

Cautiously, he moved forward and walked until dusk, then found a sheltered place behind fallen trees where he would feel safe. Again, another morning. How many had it been? He had not been marking days as he had when the slashes on his mast could be counted. Ichiro dug through his basket for some old Matsutake and herbs and continued his trek along the path.

He had walked for miles and miles or perhaps it just seemed that way in his exhausted state, when suddenly a strange sound came to him from far off but growing louder and louder as he walked along.

"Dogs!" he thought. Yes, it was the barking of dogs, more clearly now as the sounds grew nearer. Then, too quickly it seemed, those dogs were near and now he could see several of the largest dogs he had ever seen running down the forest path towards him.

Without thinking, Ichiro reached for the tree trunk nearest him and clawed his way up and out of reach of the fierce animals who were now at its base; barking and jumping, snarling, trying to reach his feet but he was quickly high enough to be safe.

How long would they stay; barking, jumping? But now, two or three of them turned and began to trot away down the path. Then, Ichiro stared in disbelief.

"Men!"

Two or three men. Wearing strange headgear, conical hats with a wide, flared base, similar to those in his own village made from spruce or cedar. They were walking up the path towards him.

They yelled at the dogs in a strange tongue; staring at Ichiro. Then, three men stood at the foot of the tree, looking up at Ichiro in the same stunned amazement as he stared back at them.

No one moved, except the dogs who now ran back along the trail. No one moved.

One man finally spoke, in a hoarse voice and in words Ichiro knew not. The man spoke again, turning to his two companions. Ichiro, frozen to the tree, only clung with all his strength and stared down at the men.

Looking fiercely at Ichiro, one of the men, with a strange woven hat pulled down over his ears, pointed to the ground and spoke sharply.

"Down?"

Slowly, Ichiro lessened his terrified grip and slid slowly down, down until he stood cowering with fear at the base of the tree. Silently, all three men stood looking at Ichiro with eyes as wide and bewildered as his must have been. One, the same one with the hat then looked at the others and spoke in short, sharp words.

Off in the distance, the dogs could be heard barking furiously at something or perhaps at nothing at all.

Ichiro picked up his basket which he had struggled out of as he climbed and continued to stand silently, ever conscious of the fierce, strong, muscular warrior before him. He stood, head down amongst the tall cedars. He had entered another world.

Chapter Sixteen

"Wun.dall!"

The large and sturdy man before him spoke, then turned to the others. Again he spoke, uttering guttural sounds that Ichiro could not decipher. Ichiro stood in shock, his first encounter with others of his own species in months. But yes, this must be some strange new land.

The men: different, and beyond anything Ichiro could imagine. They were taller than those in his homeland and much, much stockier and sturdier. Their faces, dark and glowering now as they too, stared at Ichiro in astonishment. The first man spoke again, looking now at the other two. They began to talk among themselves, occasionally glancing at Ichiro and finally the first, who seemed to be their leader, motioned to Ichiro to turn around, facing the tree.

Quickly, the man removed Ichiro's basket and although his instant reaction was to grab for his only belongings, Ichiro stood still. Having looked through his basket, the man now held Ichiro's knife in his hand, then the tanto and he looked intently at it. Next, his hand appeared with the abacus and this he looked at for a long moment, then looked questioningly at Ichiro, who just stared back in silence.

This leader now put Ichiro's knife, tanto and abacus in a loose bag from around his own hip, placed it in the basket and handed it back to Ichiro, then gestured down the pathway in the direction they had come.

"Kuhm," he spoke, turned, walked away and motioned

Ichiro to follow. As he turned down the pathway, the other two men turned and followed Ichiro. On they walked. Hours passed and Ichiro grew weak with fear and anxiety as to what his fate held in store. He had not eaten and grew still weaker, beginning to stumble and falter, when the leader turned and motioned them all to stop and sit.

The three men grabbed at sacks and bags they carried and produced handfuls of salty, dried fish, clams and mussels which they handed to Ichiro to share. There were rough strings of what seemed to be dried meats and then, a sweet, tangy handful of something dried into balls, which Ichiro knew were those tasty red berries he had picked and eaten.

The leader had been called "Gjwaal" several times by the others, so Ichiro deemed this to be his name. Gjwaal handed Ichiro a leather flask and bid him drink, then motioned to him and the others to rise and follow. On and on they strode, hour upon hour, with the landscape never changing, just the path leading ever onward and slightly downward as they walked.

Then, just as the sun which had hidden in the trees all day seemed to be disappearing and dusk penetrating the lush green forest, Ichiro felt he would collapse from exhaustion. Suddenly, a lightening of the path in front of them and they stood at the edge of the forest looking down on a scene Ichiro could hardly comprehend.

Before his eyes, huge logs and trees pushed up by the tide; a stretch of white sand, a line of seaweed, then slow rolling waves crashing ashore. But here before him, between forest and sea in a line that stretched around a bay, was a village of a dozen massive temples; the largest Ichiro had ever seen. Most were sixty feet in length or more, and perhaps half as wide.

All were facing out to sea, backs turned to the land and Ichiro would learn the sea was their world, not the land. Going into the forest was more dangerous than going to sea, for there lived wolves, cougars and the huge grizzly bears which had so frightened Ichiro.

The same grey, weathered wooden planks as on temples in his homeland, the buildings with gabled roofs, some of them with smoke rising from them. Giant ridge poles supported each roof, with vertical planks for walls reaching twenty feet into the air. And in front of each, where doorways appeared to be, were more of the terrifying trees carved into bears, whales and grimacing monsters.

Gjwaal turned and grabbed Ichiro's arm, motioned before him and led Ichiro down to the beach and along it before the temples. Before each, large boats had been pulled up to shore. Forty feet or more long, again with monsters carved fore and aft, these were the largest boats Ichiro had ever seen, although narrow and unlike boats from his own country, had no decking.

To Ichiro, it seemed that he had spent most of his life on boats; first fishing and then lost at sea. But boats like these, he had never seen. They appeared to have been carved from one, long single tree! How could this be?

As they walked down towards the end of the bay, where the largest temple stood, Ichiro realized a crowd of people were following them. Small children; shouting, pointing and laughing. Women, some holding infants, wearing long tunics, beads and ornaments in their long dark hair. Other men, glaring at him, looking mean as if challenging his right to be among them.

At the large temple, they stopped. At each end stood a tall carved pole and in the middle, the tallest pole Ichiro had seen, rising almost sixty feet into the air and carved with a magnificent group of demons, with frogs and salmon Ichiro could recognize from his own land. Carved into the middle of the pole was an opening and Gjwaal motioned to one of the men, spoke to him at length and pointed to the opening. The man, who Ichiro now knew as Skwaa entered the opening and disappeared.

Soon, Skwaa returned and motioned to them all to wait. Some of them sat, but Gjwaal turned and signaled Ichiro to stand close beside him. Minutes passed, with the crowd in silence. Then, slowly at first; a foot, a leg, then a magnificent vision of a tall man in robes, an ornate headdress, a carved stick in his left hand which he held up and shook.

It rattled and seemed to attract the attention of all gathered there and the crowd became eerily silent. Again, this man who was obviously important, their emperor perhaps... shook his rattle, then stood silently before Ichiro and Gjwaal for long moments staring, then turned, motioned them to follow and disappeared back through the door from whence he had come.

Gjwaal motioned Ichiro to follow and when he passed through the doorway and entered the large temple, Ichiro was spellbound at the vast space which was obviously home to the powerful king. Later, Ichiro would discover this was not an emperor in the usual sense, but chief of this tribe, Tlaas kwun.

Many different levels of platforms surrounded an immense open pit dug down, down into the ground, with wooden steps everywhere leading downward. Blazing away in the centre of this space was a fire, with its plume of smoke rising straight up towards the roof and disappearing through a large hole. Gathered around the fire, the long space they entered was filled with women, most sitting cross-legged on the wooden floor. Chattering away, some were weaving baskets, or were they the large conical hats some of the men wore? Children played amongst them, running along the smooth cedar boards, some shaking rattles. But, instantly all movement stopped!

Twenty or more people stood or sat, but all were staring intently at the newcomer. Children looked with curiosity towards their mothers, but all stood quietly. The chief strode over to a pile of skins, furs and mats which lay on a high platform overlooking the gathering; sat and motioned Ichiro to come before him.

"K'awuu."

Ichiro, familiar now with this word sat down in front of the chief. As he sat, the chief pointed at his own chest and loudly pronounced, "Tlaas kwun!" Several times, he repeated the word, always pointing at his chest. Then, he pointed at Ichiro's chest. Fear began to recede as Ichiro realized he was not going to be killed, sacrificed to their gods or beaten. He understood.

"Ichiro!" He spoke but found his voice still quivering with fear.

"Ichiro," he repeated and pointed to his own chest. Tlaas kwun stared intently at Ichiro for several long minutes, occasionally repeating... Ichiro... Ichiro! Looking now at Gjwaal who stood nearby he spoke again, pointing at Ichiro and listened intently as Gjwaal spoke for many long minutes. Back and forth, Gjwaal and Tlaas kwun talked, now loudly as they both pointed at Ichiro. Gjwaal also pointed outward and upward to the hills that lie behind the village and presumably explained how they had come to find their cowering prisoner.

Gjwaal then reached down and picked up Ichiro's basket from where he had placed it beside him. He showed it to Tlaas kwun and spoke rapidly and with great excitement, then handed it to the chief. Tlaas kwun reached into the bag and pulled out the abacus, looked up at Ichiro and then shrugged. Next, he pulled out Ichiro's knife and then his father's tanto but instead of just a shrug, he stared for long moments.

Tlaas kwun then reached behind him and pulled from somewhere what must have been his own knife but, wonder of wonders, the two knives were so similar it took Ichiro's breath away. Tlaas kwun stared long and hard at the two knives, spoke again and again to Gjwaal, looked piercingly at Ichiro and then put both his abacus and knife in the basket and set it behind him. The chief appeared fascinated by Ichiro.

Then, all went silent. Tlaas Kwun sat and Gjaawl approached Ichiro, took his hand and led him slowly to a platform at the furthest reaches of the vast building. He motioned him to sit, then turned away and approached the nearest woman, who with the rest, sat silently and still. Since Ichiro's arrival, an eerie quiet had enveloped the initially noisy room.

The woman stood, turned and reached into a square cedar box; one of many which lined the walls. In a pile alongside lie a stack of woven baskets of various sizes and picking one up, she reached again and again into various boxes until the basket was full. She walked slowly towards Ichiro and without looking directly at him, handed him the basket.

Recognizing at once the dried fish, seaweed, strips of dried meats, Ichiro began ravenously to eat. Head down, he ate until he could eat no more, then leaned against the wall behind him and closed his eyes. He did not intend to sleep but just to listen silently to learn what was happening; what would happen to him here in the midst of this new tribe. But, more exhausted than he had ever been, he slipped silently into oblivion.

"Ichiro! Ichiro!" A voice called to him from out of the past.

"Ichiro!" Again the voice called.

It was his mother Tsuya's voice, soft and melodious. Now in his dream, her face appeared before him. She looked at him.

"Ichiro!" And she pointed to a basket of vegetables beside him and motioned him to follow her.

Ichiro moved restlessly in his sleep, attempting to awaken and follow his mother. Finally, he sat up and opened his eyes.

Before him, not Tsuya, but a vision! Was he perhaps still asleep? Hallucinating? Where was he? But, instead of fear or fright, he relaxed into the beauty of the impossible vision that appeared before him.

Yes, he was still here in the gigantic cedar house. Sitting on the smooth cedar planks close before him was a young woman so beautiful he could not believe the glowing skin and hair.

"Ichiro," she called to him again in her soft lilting voice.

"Ichiro?" She held out to him a bowl, the usual dried fish, berries, roots of something he did not recognize.

"Yes," he answered in his own language, not knowing hers.

"Ichiro," he said quietly and pointed at his chest. The girl nodded to him.

Ichiro then pointed at her chest and then looked at her, nodding slowly. The girl looked at him questioning his actions but suddenly realized his intention. She pointed at her own chest, smiled and said, "Mu.ana."

Again, "Mu.ana."

Ichiro smiled and repeated, "Mu.ana!"

She held the bowl out towards him. Ichiro smiled broadly and took the bowl of food into his own hands.

"Yes," he nodded again and again; to the girl before him but also to himself.

"Mu.ana." Yes, he would learn their names, their language. He would become one of them; learn their customs, their ways of hunting, building the long canoes, fishing the great sea.

He was home.

In days to come, Ichiro learned there had always been rumours and myths of a race of men across the Western Sea, who have the unusual eyes of Ichiro, who know of metal, growing in gardens instead of just harvesting herbs and plants.

In coming days, months and years, Ichiro would learn that perhaps his forefathers had once visited this strange land, leaving behind some of their own artifacts and bringing others home that were foreign to his land. He would tell the chief tales and myths from old Japan of battles, and the chief will want always to know more, and wonders if someday they may sail west and conquer this strange tribe!

Chapter Seventeen

"Ichiro!"

This time it was Gjwaal who motioned Ichiro to follow him. Ichiro had eaten his bowl of food, wandered outside to relieve himself behind a wall of the great house and wandered back inside with twenty pairs of eyes following.

"Come," Gjwaal beckoned and led Ichiro once more before the great chief. Tlas Kwaan appeared to be speaking to Ichiro, but of course he knew nothing of what was being said. Others appeared and sat in a circle around them and a great discussion began taking place, with different men speaking, pointing always at Ichiro. Some spoke loudly and with great anger. One or two looked at him benignly, speaking softly. After an hour of this Tlas Kwaan nodded and turned away.

"Go.jiwaa." The chief motioned to a young man Ichiro's age who sat nearby and seemed to be carving something from a long spear of wood. The lad rose and approached the chief, who spoke to him at length.

Go.jiwaa nodded, turned to grasp Ichiro's hand and led him from the building as the chief returned to his wooden seat near the fire. Ichiro followed obediently as Go.jiwaa led him outside, stood before the house and pointed to the highest of the poles at the doorway.

"Raven," said Go.jiwaa. Over and over he repeated the word, until Ichiro finally grasped what was happening. He was in school, learning the language, the culture.

"Raven," he finally repeated, then turned and followed as

Go.jiwaa took his hand and led him down the row of houses. Outside each house, children played. Go.jiwaa would point at each child and call to them by name. Ichiro, now wise to what was happening would quickly repeat the word, the name and then be led on.

Making their way through the village, they met time and again women; sitting before a doorway with basket in hand. Go.jiwaa would point at each in turn and greet them by name. He would then point at Ichiro and speak his name. Ichiro now knew to nod at the woman and repeat her name, but with eyes lowered.

Ichiro at once noticed that as with his culture, the women seemed to be virtually silent while going about their daily chores. Watching over small children, preparing food, weaving baskets or tending fires, the women were quiet and almost invisible in the loud and tumultuous village life. Yet, as with his old world he learned in the privacy of their families that these women were a potent force for discipline and their decisions carried weight and the greatest respect.

As Go.jiwaa and Ichiro neared the last of the vast wooden buildings, they came upon a group of men encircling one of the immense canoes that were lined up along the beach, some hauled up closer to the houses. Go.jiwaa would speak each man's name, then point to Ichiro who would in turn repeat the name. It would take him weeks and weeks to remember them all.

Some of the men looked upon Ichiro with curiosity; smiling and nodding, but still others frowning and scowling. He would learn that taking in a stranger was not always looked upon as fortuitous in the village; that he might be a spy, an enemy or with his unusual countenance sent by the gods on some maleficent task.

"Ichiro!"

Months passed. Each morning Mu.ana would appear before Ichiro with his bowl of food, which varied slightly from time to time but always seemed to include some form of fish, berries; dried and fresh, and some roots or seaweed. It seemed the spot Ichiro had first been assigned had now become his home and each night the pile of robes, furs and woven blankets welcomed him before the warmth of the fire.

"Ichiro!"

Every few days, Skwaa or another brave would call him and beckon Ichiro to follow; then lead him before the great chief once again. Tlaas kwun would speak sometimes directly to him and now Ichiro could frequently recognize a word or phrase and would nod his head when appropriate.

Mostly, each day consisted of Go.jiwaa coming in the morning and leading Ichiro to the appointed work of the day. It seemed there was a mountain of fishing gear to be repaired; nets to be mended, hooks, lines, baskets to be carried or hauled from canoe to the work areas or again nets and fishing gear to be loaded on one's back and hauled down to the sea and into a waiting canoe.

One morning as Ichiro left the house to stand a moment in the warm sun outside, Mu.ana walked by with a large basket in hand. She stopped before Ichiro and smiled. He smiled back.

"Come," she beckoned and walked behind the house and up into the meadow which lie between the houses and the great forest behind.

"Berries," she motioned beneath her feet and at the side of the narrow footpath leading into the woods. She stopped and began picking, then motioned Ichiro to do the same. They spent a happy hour or two, picking the lush, fragrant red berries until both their hands and fingers but also their lips and faces were stained with the tasty juices.

Laughing, chatting, they had finally made their way to the edge of the village and were up and behind the last of the houses. Their task now led them to the grove of trees and shrubs between field and forest and once surrounded by the lush greenery, Mu.ana sat down and promptly bid Ichiro to rest. They sat in the shade and rested, while Mu.ana delved through her basket removing crushed, rotted, or discoloured berries and plunging the reddest, most delectable ones into her mouth.

Ichiro laughed. Mu.ana stopped eating, looking up at Ichiro with a strange and almost faraway distant look. He sat quietly. Slowly, her hand, red-stained and still covered in the bright red juices, reached up and touched his arm. It did not take a moment before Ichiro had encircled her with both arms and she did not resist but clung tightly to him.

Now what? Ichiro was not practiced in the arts of love. Perhaps Mu.ana was? Her face, her lips came closer and suddenly they were wildly, passionately kissing until Ichiro could almost no longer breathe. He looked closely into Mu.ana's eyes. Long they stared at each other, communicating beyond words the fullness of the feelings that had overcome them.

They kissed again and again. Often they would stop for just a moment and again connect with their eyes only, forging somehow a covenant between them; that they were now in love! Eventually, they both began to move, unfurling legs that had numbed from too much sitting, arms that had grown rigid in their tight embrace, hands and fingers that were tingling with excitement.

Ichiro breathed in deeply. Now, he was a man. He had become a man. Mu.ana only giggled as she rose, adjusted her tunic and reached for the basket. They never spoke of what had happened but in future days would find times when they could again be alone. They would approach their rendezvous at different times, from different directions; instinctively knowing they must not be found out.

All this while Go.jiwaa was teaching Ichiro the language and repeated each word, each order to him over and over. Ichiro then had to repeat the words and eventually, he was able to communicate with Go.jiwaa, with Mu.ana and even to respond to Tlaas kwun the chief's queries, in a quiet voice and with head down as the others did.

"Good morning!" Ichiro would smile broadly and now speak when each morning Mu.ana would come with food. And they began to nod, speak, smile and even laugh together. He learned that Mu.ana was Raven clan and that her mother had been a high princess of another village while her father, a chief also, had been lost at sea in a great storm.

Some days, Mu.ana would be absent, perhaps staying at a different lodge and another young woman, Aido-Wedo would instead bring Ichiro his early meal. Her brother Sgana was a close friend of Go.Jiwaa and so with time Ichiro found himself in a group of friends his age, laughing and chatting around communal fires.

Wii.lal, the father of Go.jiwaa was brother to the chief, so both were held in high esteem amongst the tribe. The first time Go.jiwaa appeared at breakfast and saw Ichiro and Mu.ana talking and laughing together, he was not pleased. Ichiro could sense his displeasure and became more and more astute at gauging just how friendly he should be with Mu.ana and she with him.

Even though it now seemed another lifetime, Ichiro still remembered the heartbreak he endured when Myumi proved to be a false friend or lover. Something in Go.jiwaa's face, his look, his posture seemed to tell Ichiro to be very wary of his behaviour with Mu.ana if Go.jiwaa might be near.

It seemed chief Tlaas kwun had delegated Go.jiwaa to accompany Ichiro throughout the day, teaching him many things, such as respect for their culture; that their tribe or village held two clans; Eagle and Raven. That intermarriage was a highly arranged affair between the clans. Although Go.jiwaa explained many times the distinctions between clans, the various villages and chiefs, Ichiro did not ever really grasp the complicated and convoluted relationships.

More importantly, much more time was spent with Ichiro learning how to work within their village culture. Houses must be built! The huge cedar trees were taken from the forest and fashioned into large planks which formed walls, floors and roofs. Other cedars would become the canoes so large that seventy men could sit and paddle.

Strangely enough, Ichiro would become renowned in the village for his skill at designing and carving the immense totems which stood in front of each house; burial poles and all manner of powerful and fantastic monuments to the tribal culture. Ichiro learned some of these totems were already a century or more old and celebrated a people and culture far more complicated and ingenious than even the ancient ways of his own people.

Today however, it was to the sea, fishing they would go.

Each morning, Ichiro gladly took his bowl of food, first savouring the berries that usually but not always arrived. Now, great quantities of blackberries and strawberries appeared and these he swallowed with great enthusiasm. More often, dried fish accompanied the meal and Ichiro was soon to learn that salmon was a staple of the diet here.

A much smaller fish, not even so tasty, the oolichan came often in his bowl and he learned over time that contact with other tribes brought thousands of the smaller fish to their village in trade, for they were not found here.

In season though, the salmon were so thick one could walk across rivers on their backs. Sea lions and sea otters were also hunted but on a good day salmon fishing with a weir built across a river, up to seven hundred salmon could be caught in their nets. Then, days of feasting would follow!

Today, however, the fish were not running up the streams and rivers, so Go.jiwaa and Ichiro joined the group of fishermen who would man the heavy canoes and journey out into open ocean. It would be one time of many the young men would spend together, with Ichiro learning to hand-fashion the fish lines made of whale sinew which they would use to catch the large salmon out at sea. Days were spent in this fashion; there was so much to learn but Go.jiwaa was generally a patient teacher.

Sharp bones were used for hooks, fashioned and carved meticulously by hand and a whole evening could be spent before the fire, slowly and carefully making one. So, today it was out to sea with line and hook.

"Hurry!" shouted Go.jiwaa as they gathered up armloads of lines, nets and enough food for the long day's hard work. Twenty to thirty canoes were lined up along the shore; two or three of the immense war canoes but mostly the smaller ones used for today's salmon run.

It was Ichiro's first time out fishing with the men; it was all new to him! So excited, he ran back and forth loading their canoe and shouting to Go.jiwaa and anyone else within range!

"Go!" he shouted.

"Faster!" He was calling to himself as much as to the others, then finally, fully loaded, he, Go.jiwaa and five or six others pushed off from shore and headed out to sea.

We.esh handed Ichiro a paddle, pushed him down into the front of the canoe and said, "Go!" Off they flew from the beach. A mile out, they stopped paddling and began to fish. The seals that dove and played soon fled the area to make room for the canoes. A small fish was put on each man's hook, then he waved it in the water.

"Ha!" Ichiro laughed. Each small bait fish actually looked like a real live fish swimming through the water and all of them caught at least eight to ten huge salmon that morning. Happy, laughing, they returned late that day to shore, knowing a communal feast would follow, with salmon roasting in the blazing fire pits and each family group celebrating the catch with drums, merriment and feasting.

Thus Ichiro learned of life upon the sea for these people; his people. So too, he was learning of life in the great forest which surrounded them.

Chapter Eighteen

"Come," motioned Gjwaal. He turned and led Ichiro out of the doorway and down, down to the beach and along it for an hour or so. They were joined by several of the other men, with Go.jiwaa, Skwaa and We.esh following.

A small stream wound its way down through the hills and forest. Here, where it entered the sea, the men stopped and surrounded Gjwaal as he spoke. He turned and the others followed as he led them up the stream a short distance, then turned along a path, barely recognizable amongst the fern and salal. Another hour of walking and suddenly without warning, Ichiro found himself again in a vast clearing beneath the massive fir, cedar and pine which grew there.

Here, many of the large trees had been fallen and lay upon the ground. All bore markings of having been chopped down with the simple stone tools used around the village, but... for what purpose? The men had all carried their bags, slung around their shoulders as usual and now all sat and drew the dried fish and meats they ate daily.

Gjwaal shared with Ichiro the food in his bag and when finished, pulled out one of the stone tools, a large axe with carved wooden handle and amazingly, a metal knife. Metal was rare here; Ichiro had not seen it in the house or village and was later amazed to learn it had come from his own country!

One day, off in the future, when Ichiro had learned enough of the language to hold forth with the chief, Tlaas kwun had told him that other men from his country had come. It had been before the lifetime of the chief but these men had sailed from somewhere far, far away; across the vast ocean. Apparently, Ichiro had the look of these men, who had brought metal knives and tools and traded them for pelts and furs of sea otters.

"Kuroshio," said Tlaas kwun.

"Kuroshio is a warm current. Flows from your land to ours."

His arm raised, he swept it in a great circle to the north and west. Had Ichiro indeed discovered this current, by wit or by chance, which had delivered him to this island and its people?

Then, even more shocking to Ichiro, Tlaas kwun told of a fishing boat which had drifted ashore after a huge storm with no one aboard. It was not from their world. Aboard, his men had found the knife Tlaas kwan often wore with his ceremonial robes. They found other metal aboard; rings and hoops, long sheaths of metal joined with sharp spikes.

"Yes!" Ichiro excitedly told Tlaas kwun that it was metal from his own land and what the strange pieces had been used for. He also learned, when the strange men came, they had worn conical hats that every person wore in Ichiro's homeland. That these men had taught youth and women in the village how to weave them. That the people had then found ways to add pictures to them; to use cedar withes, dyed with barks and plants to create ravens, eagles, salmon, and waves, then weave them into the hats.

Now, the group of men gathered before a large cedar on the edge of the clearing. All spoke excitedly, some nodded and then three of them began to hack away at the trunk a few feet above the ground. Ichiro could see that a huge cedar which lie nearby had been felled in this way; that it had been chopped, hacked, then carved into a rough semblance of a large canoe.

"Ha!" Ichiro laughed with glee! He now understood this was the work area where the men created the canoes they fished with; the massive ones they apparently used to go far asea, to visit, sometimes pillage and raid neighbouring villages. To sometimes attack and battle enemy tribes; to take women and even slaves. And now, he was part of it all.

Gjwaal handed Ichiro a strange looking tool, sharp and thick. Looking closer, Ichiro could see it was the largest shell he had ever seen; carved, trimmed and smoothed until it fit the hand perfectly, but... what was it used for? He would soon discover its great importance in the world of creating a canoe worthy of the gods!

Ichiro was now led to a canoe-shaped cedar lying nearby. Two men were scraping and shaping its bow with their tools; long sharpened bones.

"Inside," motioned Gjwaal, and Ichiro, puzzled, climbed up the tall side and into the centre of the downed tree. He still thought and felt this was a downed tree. Only later, when he had worked on it for weeks, would he see the cedar magically transformed into a war canoe.

With the sharp shell, Gjwaal showed Ichiro how to scrape away on the sides of the canoe, shaving the rough wood fibres until they lie smooth and streamlined beneath his hands. And he had done this! He was part of this; the great tradition manifesting the most prized and glorious of sea-going vessels with only the work of one's hands.

Hours passed as Ichiro happily scraped and sanded, watching also the three men who had worked their way perhaps only a foot or two through the wide trunk they were furiously attacking with their strong tools. Gjwaal and two others, including Go.jiwaa worked away on the stern and bow, fashioning... what? Ichiro at first did not recognize what was happening. The great bow would herald to their enemies just who was coming and be very afraid.

They would stop each hour or so for a drink of water from

their skins, a handful of seaweed or berries but not until the afternoon sun began to wane did they stop their labours, put away their tools and return along the darkening path to the beach.

Exhausted but happy, Ichiro entered the doorway to his home and was surprised to see Tlaas kwun rise and walk towards him. As Ichiro reached his place; his pile of mats and furs, the chief was there to greet him. Smiling broadly, he conveyed to Ichiro that he was happy with the young man's work that day.

Tlaas Kwun assured Ichiro his labour would be rewarded; that food and shelter would always be here for him in the longhouse. That Mu.ana was happy to teach him their language and that Go.jiwaa would teach him the ways of the people, the work that must be done; working in the forest where the huge trees became canoes, planks for houses and the deific totems that heralded and protected their village.

Tlaas kwun smiled and turned away, motioning to old Wii.bua who hurried over with a bowl of steaming food for Ichiro in her worn hands. His heart swelled as he felt the warmth and love of a father; Tlaas kwun who protected him. Mu.ana, who laughed with him as he stumbled over new words. Go.jiwaa, who taught him what he must know to become a man of the village and even old Wii.bua who had become his mother; nurturing and feeding him as one of her own.

Finally, Ichiro was home and happy. He ate well, lay down his head on the rolled matting, rested his weary bones and tired muscles. Ichiro slowly closed his eyes, smiled and fell asleep almost instantly.

Sometime during the night, he awoke slowly, sleepily, not knowing at first if he was dreaming or not. A few days before, he and Mu.ana had managed to slip away unseen into the woods. It had been their most intimate encounter yet. This time, Ichiro had become more emboldened by Mu.ana's sighs and moans than ever before. They signalled to him that his advances were welcome; that indeed she wished more and more passion in their kisses, more intense caresses.

Although something stopped them from consummating their hidden love; was it her slowly backing away slightly? Or perhaps Ichiro himself hesitating in their wild embrace? But he knew something had changed; that they were adults now and headed into a new time together. Where it would lead, Ichiro could not guess? A warm glow suffused him as he passed again into a deep, deep sleep.

Next morning he awoke fully rested, looking forward to the day's adventures, for in this new world, each day was a new, exciting and different adventure. For several weeks now Mu.ana had no longer come with his breakfast. So today, he joined the others as they circled the huge fire pit where food of one kind or another would be roasting or steaming.

Go.jiwaa approached him at once, excited and talking unusually quickly and then motioned towards the forest.

"We go!" he shouted and then more loudly, "We go!"

Into the world of totems, he told Ichiro. They would go with his father deep into the woods today; to a special grove of cedars where only the tallest, smoothest, straightest trees were chosen to become the wooden sentinels that stood vigil over the village, the tribe. One only would be chosen by the men of the tribe, these elders who with the chief ruled over village life.

It would take three men three days to bring down the mammoth log, days to prepare it for the long and difficult journey as it slid through the forest, pulled by a dozen young men over salal, fern and moss. Then they would place it at a junction Ichiro had seen between several of the large houses and a few smaller ones at the edge of the village. Here it would lie for weeks and months as the skilled carvers transformed the vibrant brown bark into a totem; salmon and whale, eagle and raven, frog and demon.

Finally, bark grey from the weather, smooth from hundreds of hours of sanding and peeling, the great tree would be hauled to its final resting place, where it would stand for generations in the heart of the village and before the house of an honoured family of the tribe. And today, Ichiro would become part of this, another honoured tradition of the village.

But this day, mayhem ensued. As the men gathered, tools in hand, food stashed in their bags, Wii.lal, the stern father of Go.jiwaa appeared, face glowering.

"No!" he shouted. "No!"

He approached Ichiro, stood directly in front of him and communicated strongly, over and over, that Ichiro could not come. That it was against tradition. That he was not of their clan, which was... Raven? That the heritage of their lineage was strong, was immutable, and could not be broken.

Ichiro stood silent and still throughout but now others began to mumble and whisper amongst themselves. Some nodding in agreement but others shaking their heads, frowning and still the voice of Wii.lal rose and fell in harsh commanding words. Then suddenly, as quickly as it began, he was silent.

Wii.lal stared ahead now, some of the others turned. There stood Tlaas kwun and never had Ichiro seen him look so stern and angered. Not a word was spoken. It seemed the group had almost stopped breathing and Ichiro realized then that indeed, he was holding his breath. Tlaas kwun began to speak.

He spoke for many long minutes. Much of it, Ichiro did not really understand, not only because he was a novice at their language but also because Tlaas kwun spoke of tradition, of lineage, of heritage, of history. He spoke of the traditional matrilineal lineage customs of the tribe. Ichiro knew vaguely about these customs; how vital and important they were among the tribe and the other neighbouring tribes. That they were indeed, law. No, they were *The Law*.

Yet, was Tlaas kwun contradicting these laws? Arguing against them? Was he actually speaking on Ichiro's behalf? Flouting laws and customs that had ruled the village and tribes for millennia? How could this be so?

Finally, interrupted once or twice by a cowed Wii.lal, the chief was silent but he pointed at Ichiro, then down the pathway into the forest. Tlaas kwun then turned and walked stridently down the beach towards his house. The others glanced at each other, at Ichiro, at Wii.lal, then all turned and headed into the forest.

It would take weeks, months for Ichiro to understand what had happened that day. He would have just done what he always had in the past; ask Go.jiwaa what had just transpired but was afraid that Go.jiwaa must defend his own father. From some of the others, slowly over time he learned that the felling of trees that would become monument poles was a sacred ceremony.

The carvers were not only heroes but beyond that; saints, perhaps, or deities in Ichiro's old world. The site was sacred. A stranger, member of another tribe, enemy, was never to intrude or interfere with the holy, secret and sacred ritual of their totems. And now, Tlaas kwun had overturned these traditions.

It was explained among those who sided with Tlaas kwun, with Ichiro, that Ichiro's arrival had harked back to ancient times when the strange men with the same face as Ichiro had come over the sea in their wooden boats, bringing metal, knives and wearing the same strange conical hats which were now part of their culture. Thus, Ichiro's arrival had been a portent of something new: an omen.

Those who supported Wii.lal saw Ichiro as only an interloper; an enemy. As a portent of more dangerous times, of new and unknowable battles; a hidden future. To them, Ichiro had come to represent... The Unknown.

Chapter Nineteen

One day moved into the next. Village life moved on from day to day in what Ichiro felt must be an endless stream of days; so ordered, so routinely balanced that these people had gone on for centuries in just such a manner. Only occasionally did the daily lives of the people change and this with a change of weather or season, when a run of salmon came or berries, herbs, or roots matured in the forests.

Days and months passed. Ichiro became part of that village life; learned the language, the customs, and the rituals. Go.jiwaa and he continued to work together and became good friends, although in their daily routines it was Go.jiwaa who was mentor and Ichiro student. But they laughed, worked, and celebrated together at feast times.

Ichiro had learned to never, ever glance invitingly at Mu.ana in the presence of his friend, knowing instinctively that Go.jiwaa was also a rival for her affections. Ichiro and Mu.ana were finding it more and more difficult to see each other alone. Were they being watched? The strange and fretful feeling grew and a note of fear crept into Ichiro's heart each time they met.

Yet somehow, he and Mu.ana were still able to meet secretly from time to time. Each time their lips met in a more passionate and lengthy embrace. In village life Mu.ana smiled and laughed with other young men and Ichiro, too, would laugh and flirt with several of the other village girls his age, especially the vivacious Aido-Wedo.

One morning, old Wii.bua stood before him with a bowl of fresh berries.

"She misbehave!"

The old lady spoke quietly but fiercely as she looked away to where Mu.ana and Da.a.hling, another young man and friend of Ichiro's stood together laughing and talking.

Ichiro, startled at this sudden outburst by the old lady, looked at her in surprise. Now she whispered again.

"She will marry Go.jiwaa someday."

"Not good!" She gestured to where the two still laughed together. Shocked at this new revelation, Ichiro just took the bowl from Wii.bua, sat down and began to eat.

A day later, Ichiro gathered with other young men of the village to gather firewood from the logs which drifted up on the beach or were thrown there by the fury of powerful storms. Vast quantities of wood were burned each night in the longhouses and more on the wet and chilly days so frequent in this land.

As usual, the young men laughed together, struggled together with strong branches that had blown in, long pieces of broken and split wood. Large piles of wood must be chopped with their handmade tools and carried back to the longhouses and this task took place often.

Part of the ritual of wood-gathering was the laughter, the taunting and teasing. Who could carry the most wood? Who would carry the least? The joking and rivalry went on all day; harmless banter, shouting and shoving which helped the long days of hard work pass more swiftly.

One day as they worked, Koyah began to taunt Ichiro that he came from a land of cowards; of small, weak and timid men who could not defend their women. Koyah had been one of those who resented Ichiro's welcome into the tribe and his close relationship with Tlaas kwun. All men of the tribe wished to be front and centre of those in the close circle of the chief; this gave one special and higher status in the village, regardless of who their ancestors were.

Koyah was a large and tough young man; Ichiro had always thought of him as a loud and aggressive lout! He had seen Koyah bully others smaller and quieter than himself. He did not seem to be especially talented at anything, perhaps why he was so aggressive, thought Ichiro.

This day, Koyah went beyond the usual banter, teasing and bullying. Ichiro sensed he was angry and began to unconsciously back away while trying to maintain a sense of friendliness. He grabbed a heavy block of wood nearby and headed for a pile where they were stacking larger pieces which must be chopped.

Koyah was not buying into Ichiro's trick, however. He followed Ichiro, carrying a large log himself and as Ichiro threw his down, Koyah did the same, then turned and shoved Ichiro to the ground.

"Watch it!" he yelled.

All went quiet as both Ichiro and the others knew something was going to happen. Ichiro got only part way up, then leaned on his arm and spoke to Koyah in a strong but not loud voice.

"What did I do?" asked Ichiro. "What do you want?"

Before he could rise and jump out of the way, Ichiro received a sharp kick in the leg.

"Want?" yelled Koyah.

"Want?" he repeated.

"That you work! Like the rest of us!"

"Not like a soft girl," he raged on.

Ichiro had had enough. His years of training in kenjutsu came springing back without even a conscious thought.

"Ho!" he shouted, then jumped to his feet and sprung towards the larger youth.

Koyah did not know what had happened. One moment he had lifted his foot for another kick at Ichiro and the next he was flying through the air to land unceremoniously on his backside. The other young men laughed at the sight, most having at one time or another been bullied by him.

Koyah got slowly to his feet, still trying to process what had happened but now filled with an uncontrollable rage. Not only had Ichiro somehow bested him in combat but had made him look like a fool in front of everyone who mattered: his peer group amongst the villagers.

He lunged towards Ichiro. This moment was stranger even than the previous maneuver. Ichiro danced away, turning and flipping so quickly no one could remember after what his winning moves had been. He spun and ducked, making Koyah look like the overgrown bully that he had become.

Worse, each time Koyah drew nearer in his rage and insane desire to subject Ichiro to his fist and his will, somehow the more diminutive youth rose to the challenge. Now, he was slapping Koyah at the side of the head; flipping quickly away to avoid a strike from him then just as quickly flying back to place a sharp kick on Koyah's backside.

The other young men laughed and cheered now, which enraged Koyah even more. After many minutes of this, Koyah stood still, breathing heavily and not sure how to proceed. Never had he had such an experience and never again would he. His shoulders slumped, defeat evident on his angry face.

Ichiro backed away now, appeared to bow slightly, then turned his back and proceeded to pick up the piece of wood nearby and walk away with it. Suddenly, the young men who had watched this amazing feat began to cheer. They laughed and cheered, called Ichiro by name in gleeful, happy voices. Koyah slunk away and never again would he approach Ichiro in a vengeful mood. But he had other plans.

Days passed and now another flurry of activity took place and a feast was being prepared; this time larger and of vital importance to the villagers.

"Now what?" asked Ichiro. He had enough of the language and routines of daily life that he could tell something was in the air.

"Big feast!" Go.jiwaa smiled broadly.

"Much drumming! Dancing!"

He pointed towards the doorway of Tlaas kwun's house, where Ichiro still lived; part of that family now.

"Raven!"

Go.jiwaa pointed; up and up to where the great Raven hovered over all the village, higher by far than any other of the huge carved poles.

"Feast of Raven!"

Go.jiwaa continued to chatter away as he and Ichiro joined the group of men now headed into the forest along the path towards the clearing where they worked. He spoke of other feasts, of the lineage of course, which Ichiro continued to be puzzled by.

Ichiro had heard so much about the importance of lineage; of the village heritage, of the days past, of old battles. The village of Tlaas kwun and his ancestors was apparently supreme among the local and nearby tribes. This they had done by being the bravest and most skilled warriors. The stories were endless -- of their victories over the other tribes, their voyages to far off villages where they would rob and plunder, take slaves, and vanquish whole villages.

Now, Ichiro was obsessed with old Wii.bua's remark that someday Mu.ana and Go.jiwaa would marry. As they walked along, Ichiro chatted about many village ways, asking Go.jiwaa question after question but always with the goal of understanding how or when this would happen, as the other young man and Mu.ana did not seem to be courting.

Indeed, it seemed that more and more Ichiro would see his friend talking and laughing with the flirtatious Aido-Wedo.

"Yes?" Ichiro queried as they walked along. "Someday you and Mu.ana will marry?" Go.Jiwaa glanced at Ichiro briefly, looking vaguely puzzled but did not answer for long moments.

"Yes!" he answered. "But, it is almost a formality." Now it was Ichiro's turn to look puzzled. Again, he listened as his friend explained about lineage, status, history and again, Ichiro did not really understand the complicated and convoluted traditions of his new people.

But, he gleaned from this talk... Go.jiwaa would marry Mu.ana one day and have children, as arranged even before they were born. He would then pass the lineage along to his children but that did not mean that he might not love Aido-Wedo. He smiled slyly at Ichiro, suggesting what he had guessed; that Go.jiwaa and Aido-Wedo were closer than friends! This new world was strange. It was different.

Suddenly, the path changed direction and headed upwards and to the north. "Where to?" asked Ichiro.

"Big pole," answered Go.jiwaa to Ichiro's prompting.

"Biggest pole!"

They were going this day it seemed, back to the grove to choose a tree; this one very special. The choosing of the cedar, the immense work of falling it were of utmost importance!

Before his eyes appeared, as if in a dream, the grove of poles he had come upon so long ago on his journey into the forest. A sudden shiver rattled his slender body as he recalled the frozen moment he first encountered the group of totems. Had it been part of an old abandoned village? No, apparently these people did not build away from the shore.

With a question here and there and with his difficulty with the language, Ichiro learned the grove had been in recognition of an old war that had once been fought with enemies deep in the forest. There, an honoured old chief had perished and been interred in a special burial box built high atop one of the totems. Or so Ichiro understood.

"Biggest pole!"

Go.jiwaa spoke again; loudly, suddenly awakening Ichiro out of his reveries of the past.

"Biggest pole!"

"But why?" queried Ichiro. Why would this one be different? As usual, the answers were not clear: heritage, feasting, lineage, power, authority and so on. But, Ichiro soon realized, this one was different.

"Potlatch!" Go.jiwaa grinned, shouted, waved his arms.

"Potlatch!"

So, this feast would be special. Chiefs of other villages would come, friendly and not so friendly; they would all come. Yes, Ichiro was curious but still more interested in how couples came to be. Not through love? Yearnings for each other? Could it be that he somehow would marry Mu.ana?

"Never!" thought Ichiro as he began to realize what Go.jiwaa was still explaining.

"No!"

It was not love. The young man and young woman were matched almost at birth, joined not by love and longing but by the dreaded role of lineage, of heritage; of whose great-grandfather had bested whose in some far-off battle a hundred years ago. Thus, Ichiro began to understand.

"Someday," he spoke haltingly, quietly, "you and Mu.ana will be married?"

"Yes," Go.jiwaa replied, although not with any joy or happiness.

"Yes," he went on.

"It has all been arranged."

They walked on in silence as they neared the now familiar clearing where they would take turns with the older men today; chopping, hacking at the largest tree in the grove. This giant, Ichiro learned, had been saved for decades for this time, this pole. The men worked diligently until almost dark but did not even manage to fell the giant. Back they would come tomorrow.

Soon, Ichiro realized his life had again taken a turn. Now he was an artisan; learning to be a carver, indeed he was on his way to being a master carver. In the woods, he and the men had worked away on the giant tree for many days before it was finally felled. Then many more days as the behemoth was harnessed, dragged down the pathway to the village and given a prominent spot where it would be transformed into the tallest, most powerful totem any had seen.

"Potlatch!"

Chapter Twenty

"Potlatch!"

Again and again Ichiro would hear this word in relation to the huge pole they worked on. It was to symbolize... what? Unfamiliar with the ancestry, the customs, the rituals of village life, Ichiro could only guess at the true significance of the pole.

Amazingly, he was put to work not just sanding, smoothing the pole for its final role in the village but one day Kiusta, the master and chief carver actually set Ichiro to work beginning to carve the huge monster. For monster it would be; grimacing faces of bear, whale and other fierce and startling visages glowering down at the sheepish villagers who stood reverently below, with Raven at its peak; triumphant and majestic.

Months were spent carving this pole, with Kiusta teaching and demonstrating what Ichiro was to accomplish. This must be important, for every day or so Tlaas kwun appeared to inspect their progress and comment upon it.

"Yes!"

He nodded approvingly as Ichiro held his breath almost, waiting for the day's verdict. As time passed, he saw the chief appear happier and more approving of his work. Ichiro would soon learn that indeed, he seemed to have an unusual talent for this, surpassing any other carver in the village.

"What do you think?"

As Go.jiwaa and Ichiro walked to the shore to sit with their mid-day meal, Ichiro subtly began to question his friend as to how this notoriety was viewed by his peers and the other villagers.

Go.jiwaa smiled. He was indeed happy that his friend had become so much a part of village life; one of them, that he was so honoured to be chosen to carve the special pole. That although some might be a bit jealous that they were not being recognized this way, that all had accepted his extraordinary talent and that Tlaas kwun had chosen Ichiro as a favourite.

Ichiro loved the work. Not work! It was play, at its best.

"Fun!" he shared with Mu.ana when they met.

"Have never spent days with so much fun!"

"Smoothing," he said.

"Shaping, carving!"

Mu.ana had wondered how this was so enjoyable when it seemed so demanding. But Ichiro had indeed found his calling in life. Raven, especially, spoke to him. The beak; huge and intimidating. Ichiro had found just the right look of glowering, frowning ferocity for the beak.

All those who looked upon Ichiro's work on the Raven agreed that it spoke to them; that he had created a Raven unforgettable. That his Raven symbolized the vast heritage of the tribe in a way no other native carver had ever done.

Chips of wood flew off in every direction as he worked. Ichiro ate his meals at the pole, sitting near but not on it because of his great respect for the pole, the heritage and as he sat with his bowl, dust from his work covered his clothing and often fell into the bowl.

New clothing he had now and if not for a different cast of eye, his facial structure, Ichiro looked similar to all the young men in the village. At first, he found the tunic woven from cedar to be rough on his skin, causing him to continually rub and stroke his arms and shoulders. Eventually, like with all things, he would become used to wearing something woven from tree bark and became comfortable with his tunic and robes.

Now Ichiro sat in rapture; often for hours at a time he would enter a new world of time and place. Memory would return him to that shocking yet glorious moment when he had first encountered the wooden poles; weathered trees brought to life in that forest glade. He would remember the faces which had so startled him; visages of bear, eagle, raven and whale.

Go.jiwaa and the others had over time taught him of the ancient history of their totems; the famed, now gone elder carvers who had created them. They told him of the significance of each massive creature depicted in the weathered wood. He learned through the poles the complex history of his new people; of their village and the island upon which it stood. The excitement, curiosity and strangeness of each story became visible in the features he now carved.

Sometimes, an hour would pass as he worked steadily away on the foot or two of bark before him; chipping, grinding smooth the wood within that appeared beneath his busy hands. Indeed, the quiet concentration that overcame him harkened him back to those long days in the monastery, just sitting.

However, not just sitting; another value was present here just as it had been on the mat. Some days, he would enter that precious dimension where the world stood still; where time disappeared, where he became one with the wood before him.

After these times, he would be called to eat, to return to the village and with the calling, he would awaken from his reverie to find before him, beneath him, the face of a bear so real, so awake that it would startle even him.

Where had these images come from? Had he indeed, as Tlaas

kwun once suggested, come back to the village after lifetimes away? Had he spent other previous lifetimes in the village learning to carve the now familiar beaks and wings? Who could know?

Dawn came. Ichiro awoke to a clamour and confusion that he had not known in the village. Voices shouted, children screamed amidst the melee. Everywhere was chaos; the women milling about, grabbing and holding the small ones. The men were hurriedly pulling themselves together out of sleep and rushing towards the door.

In the midst of all this mayhem, Ichiro looked towards the area where Tlaas kwan sat, slept, to see him standing bolt upright, staff in hand and face a mixture of anger and confusion.

"What? What?" Ichiro queried to the young man next to him. "What is happening?"

Gunya motioned Ichiro to be quiet and they both stood listening and looking towards the doorway where men were jostling in and out and some shouting to Tlaas kwan.

Outside along the beach, boats from another tribe were pulling in; a tribe from the North. Soon, Tlaas kwun in full regalia with staff and robes was walking towards the two boats pulling up close to shore. Just steps behind were the fiercest of his warriors. From the lead boat, which contained over twenty men, stepped another man who must also be chief. The two men approached each other as all went quiet. The chief from the North held his staff high and signalled a gesture of peace. The two men spoke.

Ichiro could understand most of the words by now, but not the full intent of the meeting of the two great ones. After long minutes, Tlaas kwun turned and walked back to his doorway and disappeared inside. The other chief turned, signalled his men to stay and followed Tlaas kwun inside.

All stood quietly for an hour or more, when finally the visitor appeared at the doorway, signalled his men and walked slowly towards the boat. Tlaas kwun also appeared, held up his hand in a gesture of peace and motioned everyone to stay quietly. The visiting chief, who Ichiro would soon learn was Lagaahl, reached the boat, turned and raised his hand to Tlaas kwun. He then turned, climbed aboard the boat, signalled his men and they paddled off with the second boat following.

Ichiro would learn that night that this tribe from the next village north, could be friend or enemy. Today, they had come as friend. Another, more warring and larger tribe from across the strait that lie to the east, had threatened Lagaahl and his tribe. War perhaps was imminent and Lagaahl had come to warn Tlaas kwun but also to enlist his help if the enemy was to attack. To this Tlaas kwun had agreed and all were at peace.

There would be no bloodletting, no taking of slaves or murder or kidnapping of women and children. As Ichiro listened to talk around the fires that night, he heard more and more of how much violence could occur amongst these tribes. How at times, it would be Tlaas kwun and his braves who attacked a quiet village, killing all who stood up to them, then taking young men and women as slaves or perhaps wounding or killing them.

Ichiro fell into an uneasy sleep, realizing that this village, although he had felt it was more sophisticated in many ways from his village; the carvings, the art, the robes, the weaving and adornment, did in fact have none of the peace and safety of his homeland. Suddenly, a thought intruded; one he had never entertained before. That his father Katsumasa had disappeared in the wars in his own country. Although Ichiro himself had never witnessed the violence of raids and war in his lifetime, yet the history of his land was also filled with war and ruin. Burned temples, destroyed families; all of this was part of him also. He slept.

Now village life became transformed in every way. A certain busyness, even oft-times a frenzy overcame the people. As days passed Ichiro would learn more and more about this special event.

"Potlatch," Go.jiwaa repeated again and again, as if this would explain everything to Ichiro. Salmon, apparently, would be the featured guest; smoked salmon, boiled salmon, cooked on rocks, the main food of the big feast. Canoes would come, war canoes carrying the bravest men, freight canoes bearing gifts, fishing canoes, women and children in canoes. But... it was all about... stature?

This elusive quality was difficult for Go.jiwaa to explain and even more difficult for Ichiro to grasp. Somehow, this feast would proclaim to the world the generosity of Tlaas kwun. Even more importantly, it would demonstrate his wealth, his stature. Gifts would be given, hundreds of gifts with the largest and most valuable to another chief. Someday that chief would host a potlatch, with gifts given, hoping to rival and even surpass those given by Tlaas kwun.

"To see families," responded Mu.ana to Ichiro's constant queries. "It is about visiting with our clans near and far. To meet with and celebrate our ties. To share our wealth, our gifts to show our love and affection."

"Strongest!" cheered Go.jiwaa, jumping up and waving his arms, flexing his muscles. To him it seemed there were different reasons for feasting; all clans getting together, friendly and not-so-friendly. "We show our strength," shouted Go.jiwaa, "to see who is stronger, we will do feats of strength!"

On a day of carving, Ichiro quietly asked Kiusta what the excitement was about and again, the answer was quite different. He knew Kiusta had the experience and maturity to have understood what it all meant.

"It is a show of power," replied Kiusta to Ichiro's questioning. "We are stronger, more prosperous. So, we will give away to those others, to show our great wealth, our cleverness, but most important, our much higher status amongst the clans."

Ichiro, knowing now the great importance of the special feast began to work more diligently on his totem, for he learned it was to be the centrepiece of this whole celebration. One day, as Tlaas kwun wandered along to admire the young man's work as he often did, he spoke words Ichiro would not forget.

"This pole will stand forever," he proclaimed proudly. "It will be a remembrance forever of this great occasion."

"This happens perhaps once in a lifetime," he added, and then smiled indulgently at Ichiro before turning to leave.

"When, when?" pressed Ichiro as he spoke with Mu.ana one day as she pressed smoked fish into baskets. With all the food being prepared Ichiro felt the great gathering must be only days away.

"Next moon," Mu.ana replied, then waved her arm in circles. "Then next moon after. Then more moon." So, it would be months until the great day?

Food. This seemed now to keep half the village in constant motion. Young women and girls were out early each day picking berries of all different kinds as they ripened. Then they must be dried and stored. Some were fashioned into the sweet balls that often graced meals and now would fill bowls at the feast.

But, with a shock, Ichiro learned amidst the fun of these days that Mu.ana was refusing for the first time to meet with him. "Come to the meadows," he implored, gesturing to the flowered fields behind the village.

"I cannot." She repeated, "I cannot!"

Ichiro is dumbstruck when he learns what is happening. "At the feast," Mu.ana told him, "at the feast."

"Tlaas kwun will announce my joining with Go.jiwaa in marriage."

"Go.jiwaa does not trust me!" she said. "He watches me now," she spoke sadly. Indeed, Ichiro had noticed whenever he and Mu.ana met casually amongst the villagers, at meal times and others, that Go.jiwaa seemed to be always nearby... watching, watching.

One day, as Ichiro and Go.jiwaa walked together towards the boats, gathering their nets to head out for the salmon runs, Go.jiwaa confided to Ichiro that his marriage with Mu.ana was imminent! Ichiro was stunned.

"But," continued his friend, "I do not wish to marry Mu.ana."

"My heart is with Aido-Wedo!"

Ichiro knew many of the young men his age were becoming intimate with the young women. It was all supposed to be a secret, but all his friends seemed to know who was with whom, sneaking off to the meadows and woods.

Go.jiwaa went on. Confessed. He was transfixed by the vibrant Aido-Wedo, that indeed, she thought she was carrying his child!

"But, but," stuttered Ichiro.

"Yes," Go.jiwaa continued. The marriage with Mu.ana would still happen. That Aido-Wedo would connect with another young man and eventually form a family. She had always known that Go.jiwaa was committed. It had all to do, again, with status, with custom, with lineage.

Only later would Ichiro understand... then why would Go.jiwaa be so jealous? Ichiro would realize that even though Go.jiwaa was spellbound by Aido-Wedo, he must marry Mu.ana and the thought that she had been intimate with someone else... with Ichiro was unconscionable! Was forbidden! Thus, as the ceremony approached that would make them man and wife Go.jiwaa became more and more aware that there must be no village gossip. No knowledge of his infatuation with Aido-Wedo. And any appearance that Ichiro had shamed him with Mu.ana was unthinkable!

Thus, Go.jiwaa had begun to watch over the movements of both Mu.ana and Ichiro. He and Mu.ana would have their ceremony with no whispers, no gossip. No knowing looks. And this would preserve Go.jiwaa's prestige with his family, his peers and with his tribe.

Ichiro's head whirled. For years, he had been among these people, now his people, but each day brought change and discomfort. Amidst his confusion, the village transformed even further.

"Potlatch!"

Everything now resonated with this word. Cedar boxes were being built, steamed, and carved in amazing numbers. Masks; some straight-faced, some frightening, some even cruel were piling up near the walls in great numbers. Tall staffs were being carved, with frog, eagle, Raven at their tip.

Ichiro, thankfully, fit into the melee with his totem finally nearing completion. Yet he sensed not all are happy with his growing status. Instinctively, Ichiro realized he must fit into this new world, if he is ever to be one with its people; to feel at home, to be home. He was met daily now with kind smiles, as those who were fascinated by his story, his history, his journey, encountered him in the bustle of daily village life.

Others, he knew, were still defiant, in complete disagreement with Tlaas kwun on Ichiro's right to live amongst them.

To all, he meets with a smile, eyes cast down if he perceives any animosity. A cheerful and clear smile to those he now recognizes as friends. Of the young men he works with, he encounters both friendly and hostile attitudes, but one day is left breathless by a sudden encounter with the reality of this new world.

Gy.aaxa, another younger man is familiar to Ichiro from their time working together in small groups, gathering firewood from the beaches, repairing damages to the canoes used every day for fishing and other of the usual daily chores.

"Ahhhhhhh!" Ichiro yells as his foot is slightly crushed when a big log rolls as they gather wood. He sits, grabs his throbbing foot and briskly rubs it. Suddenly, he is confronted by Gy.aaxa who stands before him, yelling that he must rise and work like the others; like a man. He is so aggressive that Ichiro sits in stunned silence, wondering what he had done to annoy Gy.aaxa so deeply.

Then, a moment of silence as Go.jiwaa and several other youths march up to Gy.aaxa, who in turn looks defiant but suddenly, very afraid.

"Go!" yells Go.jiwaa, turns and points towards the village. But, Gy.aaxa stands, suddenly defiant and very, very still. Someone picks up a stone and flings it, hitting Gy.aaxa in the small of the back but he just stands still. Then, so quickly that Ichiro cannot make out what is happening, three or four youths have Gy.aaxa down, are punching and hitting him. Blood is flying. Gy.aaxa is screaming in pain now. But, the fight goes on.

When finally, Gy.aaxa lies unconscious, or dead upon the beach, the others silently approach a nearby log and just continue to push and shove it, soon chatting and laughing as though everything is normal. Later, before the evening fire, Ichiro questions Go.jiwaa as to what had happened and spends the night sleepless and in shock.

"Yes!" Go.jiwaa said, his voice loud in the evening's quiet. "Gy.aaxa is a slave!"

He goes on; Gy.aaxa as a boy was kidnapped or stolen from his home and family in a village up the coast, a village of their enemy. He, like others, is a slave here in the village and must keep his head down, lest he arouse the hatred that always lingers between the slave population and the villagers. Ichiro is stunned! Is that what he is?

"No, no," reassured Go.jiwaa. Ichiro is different! He is an honoured guest... at least to most. Tlaas kwun has spoken. But it is a part of history here for the tribes to fight, sometimes for territory, sometimes other feuds. In these battles, some are killed, women taken from their children, young men and boys taken as slaves; sometimes killed. Gy.aaxa is such a one.

In coming days, when Ichiro sees the now cowering slave, he refuses to look at Ichiro or any of the others. Apparently, he has a choice. He can continue to live here, his needs for food and lodging met if his eyes are cast down and he remembers his caste as that of a slave. Or, Gy.aaxa can escape into the woods. But, he will be hunted down like prey, killed for escaping but first tortured beyond belief.

Do these intelligent people really do this wondered Ichiro? "Are these really the kind of people I will spend my life with? Raise children here?"

Ichiro learned some slaves had once stolen a smaller canoe in the night and headed north, only to be pursued for days; perhaps it was weeks until they too were finally hunted down. The longer the time of their freedom, the angrier the braves will become and the punishment much more harsh. Days of torture.

Ichiro cannot listen and turns away as Go.jiwaa continues to paint the gruesome picture of their village culture.

Something has changed, perhaps irrevocably. Ichiro will never be one of them.

Now, Ichiro's enemy is always there in the background. One day, busy with his carving, Weah nearby becomes angry with him and flares at Ichiro with his carving tool held high and just for a moment he glares straight at Ichiro. He raises his carving tool as with a weapon and his glare symbolizes his hatred. Then, still holding Ichiro's eye, Weah struck the pole with all of his strength. And Ichiro comprehends the message.

Someday, it will be him. He will feel the mighty blow of the weapon in Weah's hand or Koyah's revenge. Ichiro now knows what he must do. He will never be safe. He begins to hoard food; dried fish, mussels and clams which are being dried in quantities never before seen for the great feast which lies ahead. Dried seafood is everywhere hanging in the hot sun and Ichiro, going by, secretly fills his pouch with them.

The women and girls are picking the red, ripe berries, fashioning them into the sweet round balls that will grace the meals at the feast. All these Ichiro hoards over the weeks until he has gathered all he feels he can carry.

Chapter Twenty-One

Suddenly, Ichiro's work on the great pole had come to an abrupt halt. Although he could have spent another month smoothing the rough bark, it seemed the time had come for it to be placed in its final spot of honour. The hard labour and work required to stand the enormous pole required all the men of the village to attend; both young and old.

"Potlatch!" Again that word! The answer to Ichiro's questions to Kiusta as to why a great circle had been smoothed in the centre of the village. This pole would stand, not before a main house, but taller than any other pole, it would take that special place reserved for it over generations.

Work began. First, a strong scaffold was built. Two wings it had, with a crossbar lashed between them. Ichiro's pole was dragged with long ropes to the clearing in the village centre and every available man in the village took part. A huge pit had been dug in the clearing, deeper than those men standing in it and digging. Now the ropes were passed over the crossbar and the pole lashed to it.

Wii.lal stood in the middle of the square and shouted directions, waved his arms pointing and chanted as he led the workers in their ceremonial moves. Men pulled on the ropes, chanting in unison as the pole was raised. First, it slid down, down and the men continued to pull until it was vertical. They did this with such practiced skill that Ichiro guessed they had done it many times before. Now the hole was filled with the piles of dirt and rock which lie about.

All stood back and admired the most immense and

intricately carved pole anyone had seen. Women, children gathered to admire the work and finally, Tlaas kwun appeared in full regalia and waved his staff, first in an arc which took in all the workers; then, a direct acknowledgement of Ichiro and finally, he pointed long at the pole while the whole village cheered and shouted a victory roar. This pole would stand for millennia, long after they had all left this earth.

Again, the dawn and Ichiro awoke to yet another strange day. He could never understand what had been the cause of a sudden change in the behaviour of the people, the whole tribe. Was it the moon? Or the stars, the sea which signalled this was to be a day of feasting, of dance, of ceremony.

Before the sun had risen, voices shouted around him. There was an unusual chatter and bustle in the main hall. A noisy stirring and soon all of those nearby were busy with various chores; the women preparing food, children running out to play and Ichiro saw all of the men had left the great house.

"What is happening," he asked old Wii.bua as she passed by.

"Potlatch!" Again, that word. "Potlatch!" she repeated.

Yes, but with a few questions Ichiro learned that Potlatch would be... Today!

As he set foot outside, at once he encountered Gjwall and Ichiro stood in stunned silence. The older man's face was decorated in a ferocious mask of fierce power. His eyebrows painted, heavy and black. A half-moon decorated one cheek, the remainder of his face painted red in small squares.

Most of his body, arms and legs were painted red. Gjwall smiled as he saw the fright on Ichiro's face, then laughed loudly as Ichiro continued to stand so still in his desire to understand, to comprehend what indeed was happening.

Ichiro knew his tribe traded dried fish, carved boxes and

woven baskets to other tribes for mica from the north, used to blend the paints. Another of the more infamous northern tribes had brought red ochre from their land to be used in the random feast days. Not so random, Ichiro would learn, but celebrating old victorious battles, forays out to sea to challenge other villages and more. And today, Potlatch!

This day, in preparation for the coming feast, the men had oiled their hair; some had curled it on top of their heads, and tied the knob of hair with twigs and leaves. Some had covered their faces and heads with the white down from eagles; a very scary look! And for the first time, Ichiro saw a nose jewel; a sharp wooden stick eight inches on each side. Was this to scare enemies? It had certainly frightened Ichiro.

As Ichiro wandered through the village, he met most of those he knew but all were busily tending to preparations for the feast which would come this evening. No one paid any attention to him and he alone seemed to have no role to play in this important event.

The day was spent with the men carrying out to surround the new pole, all the gifts which the people had spent months creating. Here sat dozens of the intricately carved trunks, piles of masks leaning against every available surface. The war clubs, mighty staffs and carvings of every nature; ravens, eagles, whale and bear.

"I am busy," murmured Mu.ana as she quickly brushed past Ichiro with a huge basket filled with food. Into the great hall came women with armloads of seafood, specially prepared for the feast, while a dozen young women removed piles of personal belongings that lie scattered over the wooden floors.

By early afternoon, canoes began to arrive. Proud chiefs followed by dozens of silent warriors left their boats and strode up to the pole where they were greeted by Tlaas kwun. There he stood with his braves, holding up a massive rattle which he would shake with each greeting. Families came, children and wives and finally, near dusk a hundred people or more had gathered in the village centre.

That evening around an enormous fire, dancing began. The men wore masks, some with long moveable beaks which clacked in lively fashion. Some masks were fringed with long strands of cedar bark and Ichiro knew these were used extensively in the secret society dances of this tribe. Ichiro had never participated in those dances.

This celebration was dramatic and would continue close to dawn, Ichiro learned, with braves stomping and chanting for hours. Some wore headgear with a wide flared base, woven from spruce and cedar. Others wore carved wooden helmets inlaid with abalone shell and white fur pelts of some animal fastened to the sides and back. Ichiro had never seen anything so dramatic in his old home, or this one. But, he knew he would not be present.

For the excitement of the last few days had given him every opportunity to disappear. And this he had done, time after time, wandering off through the trees with a bag of dried seafood, berries or herbs. So light were these foods, he knew he carried days and weeks of provisions with almost no weight. Up, up the trail he had gone, hiding finally three bulging bags which he hoped might last the long journey ahead of him.

Now, at the height of the dancing, pounding drums, loud tribal shouts and songs, Ichiro would quietly slip away taking only his knife, his father's tanto and the clothes on his back. He smiled at Tlaas kwun at a special moment and then stood next to Go.jiwaa and although they did not speak, Ichiro pressed his friend's arm with affection and Go.jiwaa turned and smiled.

With Mu.ana, his parting was more filled with conflict and

when he caught her eye and smiled, she did not return the smile but looked away. Then, heaving a deep sigh, Ichiro turned and walked from the gathering. Up, up he climbed on that path now familiar to him. The first bag was hidden in trees a few minutes up the trail, the second farther along and finally, the third. Heavy they were but not unbearable and would be enough to feed him for the length of his journey home. All night he ran, until once he realized after tripping on some forest debris that he had wandered off the path in the dark.

"Yes!" Time to sleep, he thought. He awoke in the dark, his nervous thought keeping him from a restful night. Would he be followed? Would he find his boat? Would he ever strike land if he sailed out to sea? All these thoughts and more scurried through his brain and only later would he remember to stop! Not his quick movement through the forest, but the busy workings of his mind.

Up he rose, chewed a small handful of dried berries and on he ran. Water he found everywhere, small trickles beside the path, tiny ponds which lie pooled between trees. On and on, all day, when finally, he fell with exhaustion. A short sleep, on his way and then?

"Yes! Yes!" Could this be? A cairn of rocks, fallen into disarray but there in the middle of the trail. Yes, it was the last cairn he had placed on the path so many years before. Elated, energized, he ran and ran stopping only to relieve himself or eat a handful of salmon or berries. Late in the day, another cairn, another sleep and on he ran.

Was it two days and nights? Or three days and nights? Ichiro did not know and no longer cared. Every thought or experience he had ever had ran through his busy mind, driving away any fear, any thoughts of tiredness or exhaustion. Sometimes he sang and shouted greetings to any bird, deer or racoon that crossed his path.

Up, up, until one moment, sharply down and down. In the morning light he could see, now before him and not behind him, a vast sea; not waves yet, but just distance. Waves would come. Then, another dark night, pressed against a giant cedar to hide from an inquisitive bear and on awakening heard the gentle murmur of a stream.

A few steps and he was standing before it. Had he been here before? Only one way to find out and down, down he ran. Just as night fell and the sound of waves came rumbling to his ears, another cairn and he knew it was the last. He slept.

Morning and a handful of some kind of fishy thing, a few berries growing nearby and he was on his way. Yes, down, down and now he stood on warm sand with the tide rushing over his sore and tired feet. Another short rest and down the beach until he reached his cave. Through trees, branches and other debris from the pile of rocks and... there.

"Yes!" he shouted with almost insane glee. "Yes!" There was his boat. His old friend, Kaza Maru. It had not changed with time, as the few years which had passed were but a moment in the eighty to one hundred or more years of its normal lifespan. Some damage, perhaps a log had plunged in on a great tide and hit the railing but this he repaired quickly with a bit of netting tied around. The decks and rails were more weathered, a few boards would need repair but the fishing gear and nets were still where he had stashed them and looked fine.

Another short rest, a bit of food and he spent more than an hour, pushing and pushing until his old friend hit the incoming waves and slid quietly into the sea. Home. It was home and home it would take Ichiro.

Late afternoon and off Ichiro sailed into the next, always unknown part of his life. And a full life it had been for one of his years. His boat moved up and down in the familiar rhythm, lulling him to sleep just as the sun left the horizon. But, first he jumped up and hauled the sail into place. No wind now, just a gentle breeze but surely one would come. He slept.

In the night, Ichiro woke more than once. He stared at the sky, the stars so familiar to him from his last journey over the waves. He slept. Then, a sudden fear! He sat up, looking around. Something had changed. What? What? The wind had freshened. The noise that woke him was a sharp thud as the boat had changed course. It was heading now, not out to sea but swiftly to the northwest.

The next hours until dawn the boat kept sailing to the north and slightly west. Then, after a day or more of this, again a sudden turn of the boat and it swung further to the west. Now, it dipped up and down on the powerful waves and Ichiro could see in his imagination, a coast coming into view. The mountains of his homeland.

The current! The Great Current! The Kuroshio current. He had found it and was headed home. He slept.

Epilogue

A small village appeared, but only in his dreams.

A life on the sea; fishing with others.

A wife, beautiful and strong.

But, not the beauty outside to attract and mesmerize other men, but inside where it would cherish him and their family.

They would have sons, three sons.

They would be strong young men with strong names:

Go.jiwaa

Kiusta

Tlaas kwun

He was home.